THE FAR FRONTIER

The Far Frontier

WILLIAM O. STEELE

Illustrated by Paul Galdone

HARCOURT, BRACE AND COMPANY, NEW YORK

WEEKLY READER
Children's Book Club
Edition, 1961

For May Hill Arbuthnot
"Parvum non parvae amicitiae pignus—"
as Mr. Twistletree might say

THE FAR FRONTIER

One

"You ready, Tobe?" asked Mr. Evans.

Tobe nodded, spat on his hands, and bent to the log. "Heave," grunted Mr. Evans, and they lifted the tree waist-high. Then with a twist of their bodies, they hoisted it to their shoulders.

Tobe glanced at the sun. It looked well-nigh noon to him, time to eat. He reckoned he'd welcome a rest. He was dog-tired. His legs were trembly under the weight of the log and the rough bark bit into his shoulder.

The two of them moved down the slope toward the flatboat tied in the creek's mouth. Tobe put his feet down carefully, for the last time he'd stepped on a rock it had rolled under him so that he and Mr. Evans had both gone sprawling. Tobe reckoned Mr. Evans would have been bad hurt except he was so fat.

"He's got a good six inches of solid padding all around," he thought with a grin, staring at the man's round back and hips. "It must be having all them womenfolks fussing about and cooking for him."

Mr. Evans had six daughters, all ugly as a puncheon floor and full of giggles. Tobe figured Mr. Evans was building this flatboat to take them to Spanish Territory to get husbands for them. He couldn't think of any other reason why a body would want to leave the Holston River country.

Mr. Evans stepped onto the log bridge. Tobe followed him across it and onto the raft. They dropped the log at one side where Mr. Evans was building the stock pen.

Tobe watched, thankful to be idle for a minute, as the man took a locust peg and pounded it into a hole at the corner of the pen. He picked up the pod auger and bored a hole at each end of the underside of the log they'd just brought down. Then the two of them fitted it into place on the corner pegs.

Mr. Evans was going to a heap of trouble for just cow-brutes, Tobe thought. "Maybe he aims to herd them silly girls of his in here and pen 'em up," he said to himself.

Mr. Evans wiped his face and grinned at Tobe. "You and me are master workers, Tobe," he said. "We done a heap more than the Cobbs, and there's three of them."

He nodded toward the front of the flatboat, where Mr. Cobb and his two sons stood with a log resting halfway up into place, while they talked and argued. Leastways, Mr. Cobb talked. Lije and Sam just listened. Tobe figured it came of Mr. Cobb being a preacher on Sundays. He'd just naturally got in the habit of telling folks what to do.

"Sam don't hardly count; he's so little," Tobe replied.

"He's your age, ain't he?" asked Mr. Evans with a frown. "And Lije is well-nigh a man growed." He sighed, staring absently at them.

Tobe thought, "He's worried about them Cobbs boating down the river with him and his gals." And well Mr. Evans might be. The flatboat ought to have been finished and the journey started this week, while the river was still high from the rains.

Tobias Bledsoe was glad he wasn't going on that journey, through Chickamauga Indian country and all the dangerous shoals and rapids of the Tennessee. He'd sooner foot it, the way he and his family had walked to Nashville last spring and the way they'd come dragging back not ten days ago.

"Let's eat," sang out Mr. Evans.

The Cobbs dropped the log and came running. Sam and Tobe raced up the slope to the little spring and took a long drink of the icy water, and then raced back down to the river's edge, snatching and pulling at each other.

"It's too bad about Sam," grumbled Lije. "He's so frazzled out he can't hold up his end of the log, but once the work's all done, he can go legging it to the ragged end of creation."

Mr. Evans chuckled. "That's boys," he said, like

11

he had a dozen instead of all those girls. "Light and set, Tobe."

One thing about hiring out to Mr. Evans, Tobe thought, watching the man open the split-oak basket, he always brought a heap of good things to eat. Deer meat pie, a slab of thick bacon, fried apple pie, and ash cake stuffed with gobs of butter made a heap better eating than the fried mush and water he'd have got at home. He took his portion and sat with Sam and Lije among the half-green bracken.

The March day was bright and the sun was warm here where the wind couldn't hit them. The air was sweet with the smell of wet earth and fern and early green things. Two wrens hopped over the rocks at the spring, scattering the quiet with their scolding. A twig dropped into the water, and Tobe looked up to find a squirrel high in a hickory, nibbling hungrily at the big fat buds.

"He ought to work for Mr. Evans," he thought. Tree buds couldn't be half as tasty as the fried apple pie he was chewing.

Suddenly Sam nudged Tobe and said, "Looky yonder!"

Tobe wiped his mouth with his sleeve and turned. Across the creek stood a strange-looking little man in leather britches and a ragged coat.

"It's just old Asa Twistletree," snorted Lije.

Tobe stared. He'd heard a heap about old Twistletree since he'd been back here, but this was the first time he'd laid eyes on him. The stranger was a sight to see, for a fact—skinny and twisted and dried up, poking among the bushes like a 'coon after pawpaws. His metal-rimmed spectacles flashed in the sun.

"What in creation is he doing?" Tobe asked, for now the man had found a fallen tree and stripped a big piece of bark from it. He knelt, peering at the bare wood as if he'd never seen any before. His nose wasn't two inches from the tree, and he fairly wriggled as he looked and poked about with his finger.

"Likely he's a-studying ants," Mr. Evans answered.

"Studying ants!" cried Tobe. "Whatever for?" Now a body might study bear or deer to some profit. He could learn a useful thing or two about turkeys or wood pigeons. But ants! What in the nation could you find out about ants that would ever do you any good?

"I don't know whatever for," Mr. Evans answered, grinning. "But that very feller spent the livelong morning back of Haymore's cowshed lying on his belly. Mrs. Haymore, she come out and asked him what he thought he was doing, and he told her he was studying ants. She come back with a piggin of scalding water and told him straightway to take hisself off afore she poured it all over him."

"Mrs. Haymore was right," Mr. Cobb added, drawing in his chin sternly. "It wasn't fitting for her young 'uns to see a growed man making a fool

of hisself that way. The devil finds work for idle
hands, and I say his are as idle as ever I saw."

"Pappy, how about me and Tobe taking the rest
of the day to study them polliwogs over in that puddle?" inquired Sam. "Oh, I reckon a body could set
over there in the sun and learn a power from watching polliwogs gad about in the water."

He and Tobe grinned at each other, and Mr.
Evans chuckled.

"Now you boys think that's a joke," spoke out
Mr. Cobb. "But that there's just the kind of fool
notions young 'uns could get, watching that feller."

"Well, it ain't him wasting his time over bugs and

crawly things that gripes me," said Lije. "It's the
way he come down here from Philadelphy and set
himself up to be so much better'n the rest of us. He
wouldn't stay at Amis's Tavern; said it was too dirty
and fleasy."

He flung a handful of squirrel bones angrily into
the creek. "He ain't got no call to come down here
and fault us folks," he cried. "Why, me and Pappy
stayed there at Amis's twice last year, and if it's
good enough for us, it's good enough for anybody,
no matter where they're from."

"Nobody would know he was a fine feller from

Philadelphy now," Tobe thought, watching Asa Twistletree crawling around in the mud under that log.

Suddenly the stranger jumped to his feet and looked wildly around. He grabbed at something, and the next minute he disappeared among the trees, running and jumping up every few steps like a duck after a gadfly.

"Well, it's easy seen the man's not right in the head," Mr. Evans said.

"I 'low it's all that fancy schooling he's had," Mr. Cobb added. "My pap never held with book learning. Said it was an invention of the devil to keep honest folk from working. Pap, he worked right up to the day he died, and I've never seen a finer man, nor a harder working one."

Tobe nodded. He had heard it said many times that book learning gave a body flighty notions. Tobe's pappy could read the horn book and scratch out his name. But Tobe had never learned to read or write, never had time to, nor cared to. He knew a heap for a boy of eleven, just the same, how to hunt and raise a cabin and do enough farming to keep his family in corn and garden sass. Where was book learning set against such things?

"It stands to reason," Mr. Cobb said, "that if the good Lord meant for us to speak Latin and Greek, he'd have let us be born a-speaking it natural-like."

And as though that settled the matter, Mr. Evans

stood up and said, "Well, I don't mean to take up no more of my time with him. Let's get back to work."

The afternoon went by in a hurry. One reason was that Sam and Tobe were put to work stuffing mud and moss and strips of wood between the logs of the cabin, while the men and Lije lifted heavy logs into the chest-high railing at the front.

The two boys had been friends before Tobe and his family had gone to Nashville, but this was the first time they had met since Tobe had come back. "It's too bad you're leaving," he said. "Now I ain't got nobody close by to take hunting with me."

"I reckon so," Sam agreed regretfully. "But I never in my life traveled none like you. And I'm raring to get to the Spanish Territory and see what it's like."

"Well, that's one place I've never been," Tobe said, reaching into the piggin of mud for a handful. "I been a heap of other places though—Salisbury and Kentuck and over to Nashville."

"For a spell, Pappy figured on going to Nashville," Sam told him, smearing mud and grass between the logs. "Seems like every time you turn around some folks from here have gone there. What kind of place is it anyway, Tobe?"

Tobe frowned. He didn't like to think about his stay there and how another one of his pa's wild schemes had come to naught. All the worry and hard work the Bledsoes had put into that fine bottom-land farm at Nashville hadn't gained them a thing.

Oh, they'd set out with high hearts, as always, gone traipsing over to Nashville, and built a big two-room cabin and cleared some new ground. And whatever for? So his pa could trade it off for ready money to put into a wagon company for hauling skins to Alexandria over in Virginia.

The Bledsoes were a-fixing to get rich overnight, Pa had said. But there was nary a wheelwright at Nashville, and his pa couldn't get hold of any wheels anywhere close. Then somebody stole the horses. Finally it was plain that nobody wanted to pay to have skins hauled east all the way across the Blue Ridge Mountains when they could raft their own down-river to New Orleans.

So, the Bledsoes had come back east to Hawkins County with no farm, no horses, no cows, no nothing. Right this minute they were living in somebody's old deserted cabin.

"Oh, Nashville has a heap of trees and some dirt and some creeks, same as here," Tobe said finally.

"You mean it ain't no different a-tall?" asked Sam.

Tobe could see he might as well answer and be done with it. Sam was the kind of body who couldn't ever leave off once he got started.

"Oh, it's a heap different," Tobe told him, grabbing another handful of mud. "The hills there don't go up in the air, the way they do around here. They go down in the ground like doodlebug holes. A body has to be plumb careful not to fall down a hill, for it's almighty hard to climb out."

"Well, whatever for do they call 'em hills, if they ain't hills?" Sam wanted to know.

"They're hills all right," Tobe went on. "Once in a while a strong wind comes along and blows one inside out, and it stands up just like hills around here do. They're just upside-down hills, that's all."

"Aw, Tobe, how come you always got to tell a big one?" asked Sam. "How come you can't answer straight out?"

"Looky yonder, there's that old Whistlefree or whatever his name is," Tobe pointed out. They gazed up the creek bank where the man wandered among the bushes.

Lije came up then and stood a moment watching with them. "Listen, Tobe," he said. "I know a way you can get rich. Old Twistletree'll buy rocks from you."

"Buy rocks!" exclaimed Tobe. "Whatever for?"

"Well, he tried to buy one off of Abe Lemmons, for a fact," Sam put in.

But Lije said, "Hush up, Sam. Let me tell it."

Lije leaned on the log railing. "It was last week and Abe found a rock had a little sort of curly thing in it like a pig's tail. And Old High and Haughty was mighty set on having it for his own."

"Buying a rock," said Tobe in amazement. "How much did he give for it?"

Lije and Sam broke into big grins. "Oh, that's the best part about it," chortled Sam.

"He didn't aim to give hard money for it," explained Lije. "He told Abe he'd trade him for it. And you know what he wanted to trade? Latin lessons! Said he'd teach Abe to read Latin!"

Sam was giggling fit to bust. Tobe laughed too. He leaned against the cabin wall and laughed till his sides ached, at the idea of rough old Abe Lemmons learning to read Latin.

"What did he reckon Abe could do with Latin lessons?" he asked, wiping his eyes. "Skin the critters and make a pair of breeches?"

"Well, Abe told him all right," Lije went on. "Abe had a poke with him, and he held it out to old Twistletree and said, 'All right, just stuff me three, four dozen in there. My old woman will cook 'em for me.' "

Tobe laughed so hard that he had to sit down. Someone called out and the three glanced up, startled. It was Mr. Twistletree, standing on the creek bank, looking fretted.

He hollered again in his high, rasping voice. "Be there a ford here, lads? Be there a fording place?"

For a minute the three boys were silent. Then Lije leaned forward and pointed. "Right there below that rock," he yelled.

Tobe watched. He knew as well as the others that

there was a hole there. Mr. Evans had warned him about it this morning when he waded across to the flatboat.

Mr. Twistletree stepped into the water and headed straight for the hole. He went down like a rock wall and water shot up all around, sending his three-cornered hat rocking toward the boat. Sam and Lije shook silently, trying hard not to laugh out loud. But Tobe thought it was a heap funnier sight when Asa Twistletree stood up with water running off his long nose and his spectacles down under his chin. Tobe bit his lip to keep from laughing to his face.

The man didn't look at them, but floundered over where his hat had washed against the bank and climbed out.

Lije straightened his face and called out, polite-like, "Oh, I'm sorry as I can be. I must of made a mistake."

Mr. Twistletree never so much as turned in their direction. He just slapped his hat on his head, and all the water that was in it went pouring down over his neck and ears. And that did make Tobe laugh. He couldn't help it—he just busted out good and loud, it was so comical.

Asa Twistletree turned at that, his mouth all twisted and sour, and gave Tobe a look like a briar patch on a cold morning. Then he stalked off up the creek bank between the new-cut stumps.

The boys whooped and roared, Mr. Evans chuckled, and even Mr. Cobb snickered some. Tobe didn't recollect ever seeing the preacher laugh right out. They all went back to work then, and every once in a while one of them would stop and laugh and the others would join in.

"It's gitting late," said Sam suddenly. Tobe glanced up, surprised that the afternoon had gone so fast. The sky was streaked with red and gold. He'd only hired till sundown. He didn't mind working a spell past that for Mr. Evans, who was always good-hearted and didn't grudge him food, the way some men he'd worked for did. But Tobe had a good long walk home, and he'd best set out. The Cobbs began to gather up their belongings. Mr. Evans fetched his basket.

"Here, Tobe, here's a couple of them fried pies left," said Mr. Evans, placing them on the railing. "I dast not take 'em back, for my girls want me to eat every living thing they put in this here basket."

Tobe ducked his head in thanks. He knew the Evans girls packed those extra pies for him, and he could use them. It seemed like he was hungry all the time lately.

"And you tell your pa," Mr. Evans went on, "I'll likely be by there in the morning with your wage. It may be I can use you tomorrow."

Tobe wiped his muddy hands on his shirt and picked up the pies. "Well, good night all," he said, leaving the boat. He rolled up his breeches and stepped barefooted into the creek. The water was ice-cold. Asa Twistletree must have had himself a real bath, he thought, and grinned a little.

On the other side, he put his moccasins back on and took off along the trail. As he hurried along, he ate one of the pies. He'd save the other for his sister Tildy, he decided. Mean and red-headed she might be, but she could work and wrassle like a boy, and he was fond of her.

It was dark when he got home. He opened the door to the cabin and the firelight leaped out at him, warm and bright. It was home, his ma had seen to that. She'd redded up that cabin and stuck some flowers into her own grandmother's pewter noggin, polished bright as a new coin. She'd swept up the hearth and built a fire and made ash bread, and it was home before they'd even moved in good. The roof might leak and the wind squeal through the rotted away places, but anybody could see this was a place where folks lived.

Everybody in the cabin turned to look at him, his mam, and his little brothers, Charlie and Steve, his pa, and Tildy, squatting by the hearth stirring the mush. Even his oldest sister, Betsy, who hardly ever paid him any mind at all, turned to stare at him.

"I'm home," he said, not knowing what else to say with all of them looking at him like he'd grown horns and a tail since morning.

"Tobe!" screamed Charlie. "You been bound out!"

"Now hush that up," Ma said quickly. "His pa's the one to tell."

Bound out! Tobe thought it over slowly, waiting for his father to speak. It was a surprise. Somehow he'd thought his pa would always want him around to be handy, as much of the work as he did. A body might have a chance to make something of himself if he got bound out where he could learn a trade. He wouldn't mind a lick being made 'prentice to Aaron Poteet, the blacksmith—or even to Mr. Evans. But it couldn't be Mr. Evans.

Why were they all staring at him like that? Suddenly Tobe's mouth went dry and his knees felt queer. He took a step toward his father. Mr. Bledsoe had a little leather sack in his hand, and he rubbed it gently with his thumb, over and over, a faraway look on his face.

"Who to?" Tobe asked hoarsely. "Who to, Pa?"

Mr. Bledsoe got up from where he'd been sitting on the bench. In the little leather sack something clinked softly. "It was a fair bargain, Tobe," he nodded. "All hard money and a good price."

"He don't hardly see me," Tobe thought. "He's already got his head full of some wild notion or other." It didn't matter to Pa what kind of a master Tobe got or whether his boy learned a trade. It would never enter Pa's head to give his oldest son a good start in this world. No, all that mattered to Robert Bledsoe was shillings and dollars.

"Well, who is it?" Tobe cried out angrily. "The

price ain't nothing to me." He knew he'd never see a penny of it any more than he'd ever see any of his wages from Mr. Evans. What mattered most to him was whether he was being hired to some old farmer who only wanted somebody to take out his meanness on, or to a man who'd treat him decent.

"Mind your manners, boy," said Mr. Bledsoe sternly. "There's no call to holler." He put the little sack full of coins back in his shirt and sat down on the bench again. "It was a good bargain. You're hired to this feller Twistletree to go west in the morning."

The name slammed into Tobe like a blow. "I won't go," he shouted, clenching his fist. "I ain't aiming to go off with some crazy old addlebrain that don't know which end's up. I ain't fixing to make myself the laughing stock of the whole territory. I'm not going . . ."

Anger made his voice break and trail off. Mr. Bledsoe folded his arms across his chest and set his stubborn jaw.

At last he spoke. "It ain't no use to holler," he said slowly. "You got to go. A bargain's a bargain. It's done been made, and there ain't nothing you can do."

Two

Tobe squatted in the trail, watching the pack-horse eat young green cane and half listening for the return of Mr. Twistletree. He was hungry. He'd been here a good long spell. It was funny how tired and hungry a body got just doing nothing a-tall.

He heaved a great sigh. This was the dangdest thing that ever happened to anybody. Here he was hired to hunt mostly, and he couldn't shoot a lick till Mr. Twistletree gave the word. Bear, deer, 'coons, and squirrels might be all around him, and he dasn't so much as cock his piece or prime his rifle pan till Mr. Twistletree said it was all right.

Two nights out of the five since he had left home, they had gone supperless to bed, though there was game in plenty all around. There just didn't happen to be any handy at the time Mr. Twistletree figured Tobe should be hunting.

He snapped off a huckleberry twig and stuck it in his mouth. Five days and he doubted if they'd come seventy miles. Why, his sister Tildy could walk faster than that hopping on one foot with a trivet in her hand. Of course seventy miles wasn't really what they'd traveled. It was a heap more when you counted running back and forth up the trail after a bird, and crawling up and down hillsides to look at flowers, and walking back half a day's journey to pick up the saddlebag Mr. Twistletree had forgotten and left lying in the bushes.

Tobe thought about what his mother had said to him. "Make the best of it, Tobe. It ain't but six months. Mr. Twistletree ain't a bad man. And it may be you can learn something from him."

Now what could you learn from a man like this, who hardly knew which direction he was traveling?

Tobe worried a little about his ma. She had always depended on him a heap to do the heavy work when his pa was busy thinking up schemes, or to earn a little food or money when times got hard. He hoped she could get along all right without him.

He got up and eased toward his rifle leaning against a tree. There was a puffball by the tree roots and he stepped on it. It didn't even give him the satisfaction of puffing, just went limp under his foot. He stamped on it angrily. It was true; a bargain had been made and he was stuck with it. But he didn't have to like it. And he didn't have to like this bowleggedy, addlepated, book-reading, high-and-mighty he was hired out to, either.

There was a rustling close by, and Tobe looked around to see Mr. Twistletree stumbling toward the

trail, weaving in and out among the trees like a man sick with the ague. He was toting the saddlebag and it was bulging full.

When a man spends two hours rooting around in the woods and comes back with a full poke, you might think he had game in it, rabbits or 'possums, something to eat or at least worth skinning. He might have nuts, or there'd be ginseng roots to sell, or even simples like Tobe's ma was forever gathering.

But no! What Asa Twistletree had in that sack,

Tobe well knew, was leaves and seed pods and flowers, a rotten bird's egg, a dead lizard, a handful of rocks, and a ledger book.

"And that's going to make an almighty queer-tasting supper," Tobe thought gloomily.

Mr. Twistletree hung his saddlebag across the horse's back, took off his spectacles, and rubbed his face wearily. Then he peered at Tobe.

"Well, Tobias, I confess I had well-nigh forgot you," he said at last. He put his spectacles back on and looked around as though he was surprised to find trees and bushes instead of streets and houses. "Yes, well-nigh forgot you. I trust you can find us something to eat, a snippet of more than ordinary succulence. We'll camp soon."

Tobe grunted. Half the time he didn't know what Mr. Twistletree was talking about, he used such fine words. He checked his rifle and then set out the way they had come, leaving Mr. Twistletree to struggle with the horse. Tobe had seen deer sign about a quarter of a mile back, and he hoped to get one. He could smoke part of the meat that night over their campfire and pack it with them tomorrow, so they'd have food on those days when Mr. Twistletree was too busy with bugs and such to remember to let Tobe go hunting.

Mr. Twistletree was the onliest man he'd ever known who went off into the wilderness without any provisions whatsoever, without so much as a dab of salt or a handful of meal. "And him a city

body with only an old fowling piece to shoot with too," Tobe thought. He didn't know what the man would have done without him.

Suddenly in the trail right in front of him he spied a big turkey, stepping along with its head up like it was going to Salisbury to lay claim to the whole state of Carolina. Almost without thinking, Tobe raised his rifle and shot. The turkey dropped into the trail and flopped around a few times before it lay still.

Behind Tobe, Mr. Twistletree's rasping voice called out, "Fine shot, boy."

Tobe scowled. "I don't need him to tell me what's a good shot," he muttered. He pushed back the frizzen and sprinkled powder from his horn over the touchhole. Did Asa Twistletree think that because he couldn't read he couldn't hit a sitting turkey cock? He'd been shooting a rifle for years now. His father was always too busy getting rich to do much hunting, so it was a task that had fallen to Tobe long ago.

He finished loading the gun and shot the ramrod home in its thimbles underneath the barrel. Then he picked up the bird and sliced its head off with his hunting knife to let the blood drain. He would have liked to go after that deer, but it was late and there was a heap to do nursing old Twistletree.

His master led the way down the trail, but it was Tobe who had to point out a little hollow to one side where there was a spring.

"Won't find no better place," he said. "It's fixing to get up a wind tonight. We'll need to be down there out of it."

"Yes, a wind." Mr. Twistletree nodded. "The Equinox is upon us, when the four corners of heaven send forth their breath to whistle up the warmth of spring."

Tobe was exasperated. "Do you aim to camp here or not?" he cried.

"Why, surely, Tobias," Mr. Twistletree answered mildly. "I find your judgment excellent in these matters."

Tobe took the lead line and jerked the horse off the trail. Sulkily he led the way into the hollow. He unloaded the horse and hobbled it, fetched water, built the fire, and gutted the turkey, while Mr. Twistletree sat on a log and watched some beetles.

Presently the man took out his ledger book, ink horn and quill, and began to write. He looked back at the beetles, stood up to see them better, and sat down on the book. He watched the beetles for a spell and then searched around him for his book.

Tobe, plucking the turkey, said nothing.

Frowning, Mr. Twistletree muttered to himself and pawed around behind the log. "Have you seen my ledger, Tobias?" he inquired at last.

Tobe flung down a handful of feathers. "You're a-setting on it," he answered and ducked his head to grin.

Mr. Twistletree was delighted. "I was afraid I'd lost it," he told Tobe, getting up.

Tobe finished plucking the bird and spitted it over the fire. One good thing, he told himself, he'd have a heap to tell his mam and Tildy and the others when he got back. They'd find it hard to believe a man could be as feather-headed as Mr. Twistletree all the time.

And oh, wouldn't he give a pretty to have a chance to tell Sam and Lije Cobb about what had happened this morning! Tobe had no more than set out with the horse at his heels when Mr. Twistletree had spied a bunch of little new toads in the trail. He'd thrown himself flat on his belly and lain there, just like that time behind the Haymores' cowshed, never moving a muscle, just watching those little hoppers as hard as he could.

Tobe had sat down at the trail's edge to wait. He heard the folks coming a long time before they got there, but he hadn't said a word to Mr. Twistletree. He reckoned it must be a whole mess of folks, for they made enough noise to wake the dead.

The travelers had come up to them, and the first horse all but stepped on Mr. Twistletree before he started to scramble up, red in the face.

"I . . . I beg pardon," he stammered, still on his knees. Part of his coat was caught under him and every time he tried to stand, he jerked himself back down. "I . . . I . . ."

"Be he having a fit?" the man on the first horse asked Tobe.

"Naw," answered Tobe briefly. He wished now he'd hollered at Mr. Twistletree to get up sooner. Anybody could see the two of them were traveling together. These folks would think he was as doty as Asa Twistletree.

"He looks bad off to me," a woman stated, urging her horse up closer.

"Is he fitified?" sang out somebody at the rear of the line.

"Boy says he ain't ailing," the leader said.

"Well, get him outa the way then," the man yelled. "We're in a hurry to get to Nashville."

The leader edged his horse forward, and Mr. Twistletree turned white. "The toads," he said with a groan, wringing his hands, lurching up out of the way. "Watch out for the toads."

But the folks hurried on past, men with rifles and oys Tobe's own age riding horses loaded with verlids and pots and pans, and one or two women-s. They all stared at Mr. Twistletree, some of t. m grinning, some of them angry. And all the ti... he was shooing the toads out of the way and straightening his glasses and waving his arms about, so that he scared most nigh every horse that passed.

When they had gone, Mr. Twistletree had found one of the little toads mashed into the dirt. The rest were nowhere to be seen. It tickled Tobe yet to think of the way the man had clicked his tongue over the critters as though he'd lost something worth money.

Now Tobe added more wood to the fire and turned the turkey a little, sniffing with pleasure the mixed smell of wood smoke and browning meat. It would be a good while cooking, but he didn't know as he'd wait that long. Half-cooked was fine, hungry as he was this night. And Mr. Twistletree wouldn't eat but the least little bite anyway. Tobe had never seen a man who cared so little about what he ate, who'd just as soon as not go to bed without.

Tobe shrugged. "There's more for me if he don't eat."

That night the wind rose, as Tobe had said it would. Chill and sharp it howled over the little hollow, and in the morning there was a powdering of snow over everything. Tobe took a deep breath and felt the sweet cold air burn down into his chest. Oh, he'd a heap rather be out here in the woods than in a blacksmith's shop, and that was the truth. He might not be learning a trade, but in the spring of the year it was better to be out under the shagbark hickories and poplars than bending over an anvil.

The sun came up and melted the snow, leaving only what was in the shade, so that the trees cast long white shadows that slowly melted like candles from the top down. Far off Tobe heard geese honking, a-gabbling about getting up and moving north, maybe.

That day they reached the Clinch River, and it startled Tobe to see how ugly and swollen it was.

It hadn't been this high when the Bledsoes had crossed here almost a month ago coming back from Nashville. Now it went roaring along waving little foamy ripples over the rock where he stood. He didn't like the look of it. He'd never in this world be able to get Mr. Twistletree across. Useless as the man was on land, he'd be twice as bad on a wobbling raft. And he wasn't sure that the old boney nag could make it either, for she'd not had proper care before somebody had deceived Mr. Twistletree into buying her.

Tobe shook his head. They might best wait till tomorrow. It could fall a lot overnight, and he'd learned a long time ago not to treat a river in flood lightly.

"Have you a penny for Charon?" asked Mr. Twistletree absently.

"What?" asked Tobe.

"Nothing," replied the man. "You'd best cut cane, boy."

"Whatever for?" Tobe wanted to know.

"To raft our belongings over," explained Mr. Twistletree. "Rope and cane—you couldn't ask for anything better."

"A raft out of a bundle of canes!" Tobe cried angrily. Only a helpless niddy-noddy like Mr. Twistletree would think you could cross a river on a bunch of canes. "It won't never hold us up. Lessen you want to lose every smidgin thing we got, we'd best make a log raft."

"It ain't supposed to hold *us* up," Mr. Twistle-tree replied. "Just our worldly goods and meager possessions. And you're supposed to hang on behind and kick your legs a mite; that's all you have to do."

Tobe was silent, thinking this over. "What about you?" he asked sullenly. "What do you aim to hang on to?"

"Oh, I'll ride the horse," Mr. Twistletree answered in some surprise.

"The horse!" repeated Tobe.

"Why, yes," replied Mr. Twistletree soberly. "I've had my wetting for this week. Do you not recall the creek where you were building a flatboat?"

Tobe flushed and looked away. It was the first time Mr. Twistletree had mentioned the trick they'd played on him. Tobe had figured he'd forgot it or maybe didn't recognize him. It was underhanded to wait till now to mention it.

The boy stood there uncertain, watching the waters swirl by, giddy and swift.

"Boy, you ain't scared?" the man asked.

"Naw," Tobe answered quickly. "I ain't scared."

He jerked his tomahawk from his belt and hacked away. He laid into that cane with a right good will. Mr. Twistletree had no call to name him a coward. Only a light head would go in that river holding onto a piece of cane without giving it some thought.

Tobe cut a heap of cane, and he used the horse's ropes to tie it into bundles. Then he lashed the bun-

37

dles together with their belongings on top. He wrapped one blanket around his rifle and the old fowling piece Mr. Twistletree had brought along, the other around the powder and lead. When everything was secure, he began to take off his clothes.

Mr. Twistletree mounted the horse and turned to look down at Tobe. "You'll be all right," he assured the boy. "Just kick a little to keep yourself afloat."

He rode down the bank and into the river. Tobe saw the horse stagger when the current hit it, and for one moment Tobe thought Mr. Twistletree was a goner. But the animal began to swim. Mr. Twistletree had wrapped his ledger and pen and ink in his great coat. These he clutched to his chest to keep dry, although the water only came to his thighs.

By the time Tobe had finished undressing and stuck his clothes under one of the ropes, the man and horse were safely across. Tobe pushed the raft off the sloping rock. It settled in the water and wobbled fiercely. He eyed it uneasily. He wasn't what you might call a swimmer.

Of course it had been a heap easier than making a log raft, for a fact, and quicker. "But quick and easy don't mean safe," he said to himself. He poked at the contraption, dreading to start.

Well, he couldn't stay here all afternoon. What he had to do, his master had already let him know. He splashed in and stood a minute by the raft. The water was cold enough to freeze bear grease.

He thought he heard a shout from across the stream.

"What's his hurry?" he asked aloud. "He ain't been in any hurry up to now."

✓ Angrily he shoved the craft out into the river and plunged after it, holding tightly to one corner. The current caught the raft and it dipped, for all the world like it was sinking straight to the bottom. Tobe kicked out with both feet in a panic.

But the cane didn't sink. It floated light and fine. And Tobe kept kicking, anxious to reach the other side. His legs began to tingle with the cold. The icy water, pressed against his stomach and chest, squeezed him so he couldn't seem to get his breath properly. But he'd almost reached the other side and there was Mr. Twistletree watching.

He drew up his legs to kick again. And then suddenly he couldn't kick. His legs were knotted up, tight as a gun spring, and they couldn't straighten out. A pain welled up in his right leg. Big as a barn, it felt like. It twisted and twisted, till he was sure his muscles were going to snap in two. He gasped and let go of the raft, reaching for his aching leg.

✓ He was sinking. He grabbed for the raft, but the current had sent it spinning off downstream, out of reach. His head went under.

Three

Tobe went down in the icy water like a stone. His numb hands clawed at his twisted leg and the iron pain of the cramp. He sank till something exploded in his head like the bright flash of gunpowder. Strange shapes and colors floated before his eyes and weird voices gurgled in his ears.

"I'm a-drowning," he thought.

He was astonished. He, Tobias Bledsoe, a big able-bodied, level-headed boy was drowning in the black Clinch River like any knucklehead. He tried to fling out his arms and grab something, anything at all. But there was a great dead weight on his shoulders and his arms were too heavy to move. The water was as thick and gummy as honey. It pressed in on him from every side, tighter and tighter, and he began to spin slowly around.

Then something grabbed him by his hair. Something hauled him up and out into the air, and he coughed and choked. He struggled to get his breath, flinging his arms wide and clutching as if he might grab more air to him. But it seemed as though all he could do was gag and splutter.

"Hold still, Tobias," squeaked Mr. Twistletree in his ear.

Then he felt the ground under his feet, and Mr. Twistletree pulled him up the bank and turned him on his chest and gave him a good lick between the shoulder blades that sent most of the water slopping out of his mouth. He rubbed and kneaded Tobias's leg with his small strong hands till he all but peeled the boy's skin off. At last the cramp untied itself, and Tobe sighed and stretched out his leg.

Mr. Twistletree covered him with the great coat. "Now be still, Tobias, and I'll make a fire. We both must dry out."

Aching and shivering, Tobe huddled down inside the coat. He could feel his cold wet arms pressed against his cold naked sides. He'd never get warm, never, never. Over the chattering of his teeth he could hear Mr. Twistletree moving about and the dry papery sound of leaves, the sharp snaps of twigs. His heart beat slowly and heavily. He closed his eyes and fell into a kind of stupor.

Suddenly he gave a start and sat up. Mr. Twistletree was down on his knees beside a smoking heap of leaves, coughing and trying to blow up a fire at the same time. Every time he puffed at the heap of brush, smoke flew up into his face, and he would begin to snort and splutter.

He sneezed and the smoking leaves scattered

every which way. Patiently he gathered the leaves into a pile again, crumbled on some dead wood, and dropped to his knees. He took his flint and steel and began to click them together.

It'd be a lucky spark that ever hit and caught in the leaves that way, Tobe thought. He ought to tell him how to do it. He felt so heavy and cold, he didn't think he could. But why would a grown man need to be told how to make a fire? It was enough to try the patience of a toad.

"Get you a fistful of dry grass to catch the spark," Tobe spoke out at last. His voice sounded hollow and strange, as though it was some other boy speaking.

Mr. Twistletree looked up with his eyes watering and red from the smoke. He nodded and got up and fetched some grass from the riverbank. This time he got down close to the grass and kept steadily at work, scraping the flint and steel together till he had the grass blazing. And even then he almost put the flame out, throwing a lot of leaves down on top of it.

"Put the coat on and come close now, Tobias," Mr. Twistletree commanded.

Tobe did as he was told, but just to stand up and slip his arms into the sleeves made him shake so that he all but fell flat. Holding the coat around him, he managed to drag himself over beside the fire. His face tingled as the leaves caught and blazed up hot and bright.

Mr. Twistletree stood across from Tobe, rubbing his hands together, staring into the flames over his clouded spectacles. He stayed like that till the fire had well nigh burned itself out, then went hopping around looking for something else to put on it. What he found was mostly leaves, which burned up as fast as he came up with an armful and threw them on.

Winded at last, he stood looking helplessly around. "Fie on it," he said. "I need my ax."

Tobe raised his heavy lids. He was feeling better. He'd give a silver shilling for a gourd full of hot goose-grease to rub into his sore leg. But he reckoned he'd live without it.

And right now something had to be done about the fire. He didn't want to see Mr. Twistletree go through all that business again. The man was right this minute kicking at an old water-soaked log trying to break off a piece to put on the blaze.

"That'll be no more help than spitting on the fire," Tobe figured.

He got up and dragged himself over to a big shagbark hickory. He stripped off an armful of the curly bark and brought it back and laid it on the fire.

Moving around made him cough, and his legs sagged under him. He sank down on the ground and rested his head in his hands.

"I thank you, Tobias," said Mr. Twistletree. "I

thank you very humbly for helping with the fire when you are in no fit condition. You see now why I am forced to hire some lad to go with me into the wilderness."

He smiled. "There was a time I fancied any man of intelligence could make his way in the woods. But it isn't true. It takes a skill I do not have and can never acquire I fear."

He shook his head and Tobe was astounded. You'd think if a body was so backward at simple things like making a fire, he would be too shamed to talk about it.

Mr. Twistletree took off his linsey shirt and held it close to the flames. "Oh indeed, yes," he went on. "Twice I've been on a journey like this alone. But the last time, I fell ill—mostly because I so often forgot to eat, but also because I couldn't build a proper fire, and many a night I slept wet and cold to the marrowbone."

He sighed and turned the shirt the other way. Tobe stared at the man's skinny chest and meatless ribs. Mr. Twistletree was queer as Dick's hatband. How in thunderation could anybody forget to eat? No wonder he was so thin that he hardly cast a respectable shadow.

"It was my sister in Philadelphia who made me agree to take a helper with me," he told Tobe. "Twice I went with a lad from Penn's state, a good enough boy, handy with an ax or a gun. But he was stupid. Sullen and bone-headed. This time I aimed to find a young man with brains to be my companion."

He put his shirt back on and half stuffed the tail into his breeches. The rest trailed behind him forlornly as he twirled and twisted before the fire to dry his breeches.

"You, Tobias, now you are a bright lad."

"Thanky," muttered Tobe.

It made him uneasy to have the man praise him, and he was a mite suspicious. Whatever for would Mr. Twistletree come into the wilderness, seeing he was so unsuited for it? How come he didn't stay back in Philadelphia where he wouldn't have to struggle with his own fire or shoot his own dinner or even have to remember to eat it?

Tobe shook his head. He'd never make sense out of this man. Mr. Twistletree was like a man with three crooked legs or with his head all screwed on wrong so that his face turned around backward. He was just so different from the rest of the world, a body couldn't hope to ever figure him out.

Tobe stood up finally. "We'd best go look for that raft," he said. He was worried about his rifle and other gear.

"Not you, Tobias, not you," cried Mr. Twistletree. "You stay here, and I'll sally forth and fetch our belongings back. You ain't fit yet."

"I'm fine," said Tobe doggedly. He wasn't. His legs ached and trembled still, but he knew in his bones Mr. Twistletree would leave him to sit by the fire for hours while he wandered along the river's edge, likely forgetting to look for the raft at all.

They set out. Tobe couldn't help grinning to himself. They must make a pretty pair, skinny Mr. Twistletree running along in his patched linsey shirt, with his spectacles askew and his hair on end, and Tobe in nothing but the flapping great coat.

Right off, Mr. Twistletree found a bird's nest in some brambles. He shook it gently and a meadow mouse ran out. Her tawny back and white undersides gleamed in the sun, and Tobe caught a glimpse of her naked babies clinging to her.

"Oh, a pretty creature," murmured Mr. Twistletree. "And I have heard that she acquires not only the house of a bird, but a bird's very nature, and can sing as sweetly as any nightingale."

Tobe shrugged and walked on. Mr. Twistletree would sit there for the rest of the day waiting for this mouse to sing to him. It angered Tobe to think that as bad off as they were for their belongings, the man could waste time like that.

He stumbled along the river's edge, hoping any minute to find the cane-bundle raft on some rocky bar or caught behind some half-drowned tree with the flood trash. It couldn't have gone much farther than this surely.

Had he missed it? He looked back the way he'd come, heavy-hearted, not knowing whether to keep on downstream or not. But he knew he hadn't passed

47

it by. He'd checked every bulged-out piece of land and every stuck-in piece of river, and it just wasn't there.

Had the raft sunk? Had his rifle and his clothes and every other thing he owned been strewn over all the river bottoms between here and the Ohio? He groaned to himself. This was the kind of thing that happened to folks who went with a natural-born dern fool like Asa Twistletree.

But he was too tired and sore to lose his temper. Besides, what was done, was done. There wasn't any more use blaming Mr. Twistletree for the stupid cane raft than there was in faulting his father for binding him out. But the man could at least help look for the tarnal thing. The blanket and cooking pot belonged to him, and there was his old fowling piece and all his bird skins and rats' tails.

"But no, *he'd* rather worry and poke at some mouse creature than look after his truck," Tobe remarked bitterly.

He rubbed his aching leg and limped off downstream once more. Here the river had gone out of its banks and rushed over a pebbly beach thick with button bushes. Somebody was sloshing around among the bushes and Tobe was surprised. How in the nation had Mr. Twistletree got ahead of him without his knowing?

"Mr. Twistletree!" he shouted and limped forward in the shallow water.

And then he stopped. Whoever that was among

the button bushes, it wasn't Asa Twistletree. It was some big broad-backed body with a thick red neck and a dirty deerhide shirt.

The man stood up then and turned around to face Tobe. He was a mean-looking critter with squinting black eyes. He gripped a rifle under his left arm and another gun in his right hand. He held this one up to show Tobe.

"Looky what I got," he exclaimed. "A right fine rifle just throwed away in the bushes."

"It ain't throwed away," Tobe cried out. "It got carried off by the river. It's my rifle. Give it back."

He ran up and grabbed at the gun, but the stranger held it over his head out of reach.

"I found it," the man said curtly. "You ain't got no claim a-tall to it now. It ain't every day a man finds a good rifle in the bushes, and I don't mean to let it go. It's my rifle now and you can whistle for it!"

He raised the butt of the other gun and gave Tobe a hard shove.

Four

Tobe staggered back among the button bushes and crouched there glaring at the thief. He watched the man unwrap the piece of greased deerhide from around the gun lock, cock the hammer, and pull the trigger to see how it worked. The stranger checked the muzzle to see if it was pitted from powder burns and seemed mighty pleased with the rifle.

Anger made Tobe tremble all over. "If'n I was just a mite bigger," he groaned to himself. "If'n I hadn't just well-nigh drowned and got this fierce knot in my leg, I'd give that feller a beating he wouldn't forget in a hurry. I'd whomp him a good one and then I'd take his old fool gun and wrap the barrel around his neck good and tight till he hollered calf and . . ."

He stopped. He wasn't bigger. He was so weak and wobbly he couldn't stand up to a groundhog, much less to a strong full-grown man. His only chance would be to grab the rifle and then run like a cane brake afire. He didn't think he could do even that, but he aimed to try. It was a heap better to try something than to squat here silently and let a man steal his good rifle.

He stood up and pushed back the sleeves of the great coat. The man paid him no mind. Tobe began to edge slowly toward him.

Suddenly the man jerked around. "Now you just stay put, right where you be," he said, and his voice was hatchet-sharp. "Do you start something, I'll stomp the liver and lights out of you."

He would too, Tobe knew. He stepped back among the button bushes, and his mouth filled with the sour taste of despair. "A body might as well have a hand cut off as lose his gun," he thought grimly. And his rifle was the onliest thing in the wide world that was truly his. He'd earned it himself, trapping beaver for furs, grubbing up ginseng roots, doing every least last thing he could think of to make a penny. It had taken a long time and a heap of hard work, but it was his, every frazzling bit of it.

He'd kept it greased and clean as a pin, worried with it night and day, made a new stock of red curly maple, and now he had him a pretty fair gun all around. He could kill a deer as easy as most folks picked up persimmons.

With a last look at his rifle, he turned away and walked slowly back along the riverbank. He found Mr. Twistletree not far from where he had left him. The man was down on his hands and knees

now, looking at a big orange fungus growing out of a rotten log.

He glanced up when he heard Tobe. "Did you find the raft?" he asked, twisting his neck and squinting his face behind the spectacles.

Tobe nodded gloomily. A boy out in the woods with a man might in reason expect the man to lend him a hand, to help him out when some thieving scoundrel ran off with his rifle. But he, Tobe, was out here with Mr. Twistletree, this skinny half-witted fellow with his shirttail trailing behind him and his hat over one ear. He couldn't hope for any help from this man. Asa Twistletree was no more good to him than a bullet mold would be to a red-headed peckerwood.

"I found it," he said heavily. "But somebody got to it before me. Some old woodsy done found it, and he's fixing to go off with my gun!"

Mr. Twistletree stood up slowly. "I should have gone after the raft sooner," he muttered. "I never thought there would be anyone about to steal our things."

"He ain't stealing *our* things," Tobe told him fiercely. "He don't want them fleasy blankets or that skillet with one leg broke or them puny little bird skins. Likely even the powder has got wet. What he wants is *my* good rifle. If'n I had another gun, I'd shoot him."

"Hush, boy," said Mr. Twistletree. "There's no call to lose your temper. Out here in the woods finders are keepers. Come along now and keep quiet."

Tobe walked along behind his master. The great coat swished about his knees. What did old Twistletree plan to do, he wondered scornfully? Lay hold of that feller and squeeze him till he spit out the rifle? Or maybe speak in Greek and scare the woodsy out of his moccasins?

They came to the pebbly beach, and the woodsy was still there turning over the things from the raft with his foot. Tobe saw his patched deerhide shirt and breeches, floating in the water.

"How do you do?" asked Mr. Twistletree, and his voice was harsher than ever.

The other man grunted and kicked disgustedly at the wallet of powder. He didn't even trouble to glance up.

"I see you have two rifles," Mr. Twistletree went on. "I am in need of a good firearm. Would you be willing to sell?"

Tobe opened his mouth in horrified surprise. Buy back his own rifle! Whoever heard of such wickedness?

The man turned, slanting around slowly. He looked Asa Twistletree up and down and grinned. It was an ugly grin. He reached down to the raft and held up the old fowling piece. "How about this here one?" he asked. "I'd part with it willing."

Mr. Twistletree shook his head impatiently. "No,

no," he cried. "I am in need of a decent rifle. Something for killing game."

The man shrugged. "Well, you don't want it," he said, looking the fowling piece over. "And I don't want it. Reckon I'll just fling it away."

He hurled Mr. Twistletree's gun over the bushes. Tobe could hear it splash into the river. He gave a strangled yelp and lunged forward. It might be his rifle next.

But Mr. Twistletree grabbed him by the arm. "Be quiet, Tobias," he commanded.

Tobe stared at him. Asa Twistletree must be cold as a fish to let a rascal like this make sport of him and never raise voice nor hand.

"Would you sell one of the rifles?" Mr. Twistletree asked evenly.

The other man pondered. He gazed off into the distance for a long time, rubbed his stubbly chin, and finally spat into the water by Tobe's feet.

"I'd have to get a pretty fair trade," he said at last. "I wouldn't part with this 'un," he went on, holding up his own weapon. "But this here 'un"— he gave Tobe's rifle a little shake—"I might be sweet-talked into selling. I'd have to get a good price for it howsomever. It was my daddy's old rifle."

"That's a lie," Tobe blurted out in spite of himself. He was dizzy with rage and he staggered on his trembling legs. Mr. Twistletree steadied him, digging sharp fingers into his shoulder.

The woodsy looked them over again. His eyes were shrewd and calculating. "I just might trade at that," he told them. "I reckon this rifle's worth a good riding beast."

Tobe wanted to tell Mr. Twistletree to take it and be quick about it. His gun was worth a heap more than that bony old nag any day.

"The boy and I are afoot," said Mr. Twistletree easily.

Tobe pricked up his ears a little. Who would have thought old Twistletree could tell a lie like that without so much as batting an eye?

"No," went on Mr. Twistletree smoothly, "money is all I have to trade. I will pay a fair price for a rifle, but that's all."

The man grinned a little. "Six silver shillings I'll take for this rifle, and no less," he added.

Mr. Twistletree tightened his grip on Tobe's arm. He shook his head firmly and made as if to turn away. "No, I'll do without. Likely so old a gun would have a rusty barrel. I couldn't give more than three shillings."

It made mighty pretty talk, Tobe thought, staring at his companion to see if he meant it, for where under the sun would Asa Twistletree get three shillings? Hadn't he said he'd given Mr. Bledsoe all the money he had for Tobe's hire?

The woodsy squinted. "Oh, this is a fine piece," he exclaimed. "Nary a screw or a spring out of place. It's been took care of good; you can take my word for it. It's sure worth the money." He looked down at Tobe's gun. "But I'd hate to think of a fine feller like you out here in the woods without no rifle. I'll take four shillings."

Asa Twistletree shrugged, unconcerned. "Very well," he said. "Four shillings it'll have to be, for that is all I have in the world, and I need a rifle."

Tobe jerked away then and sprang forward to grab his rifle, but the stranger cuffed him aside. "I never sold it to you," he snarled.

Tobe stayed there trembling, afraid Mr. Twistletree couldn't find the money and the woodsy would go his way with the gun. The little man pushed up his spectacles and took forever to search his pockets. Tobe bit his lips and the woodsy's eyes got hard as flint as he waited.

Just then Mr. Twistletree held out his hand and the sun glinted on the coins. The woodsy snatched the silver and shoved the rifle into Mr. Twistletree's hands. He bit each piece to make sure it was good and slipped them inside his shirt.

"I'll drink to your health and good fortune at Jonesboro," he sneered and swaggered past them into the bushes.

Tobe made a growling noise in his throat. "I'll kill that feller if'n I ever meet him again," he promised himself.

"Come 'long, Tobias," said Mr. Twistletree. "We'll find our bits and pieces and get back to our camping place." He held out the rifle and Tobe reached for it. Then suddenly he drew back.

"Naw," he muttered, half turning away. "It ain't mine no more. It's yourn. You paid for it."

"Fiddlefab!" cried Mr. Twistletree. "I'm responsible for your possessions while you're in my hire. You must have your rifle." He pressed it firmly into the boy's hands.

Tobe looked down at the gun. He'd have to take it. He'd been hired to shoot game. But he'd have to handle it like it was a borrowed gun. He wouldn't ever feel the same about it, not ever.

He was wrong. As soon as he took it and felt its comforting weight in his hands, it was the same as always, as though it had not been lost to him at all, nor could ever belong to anybody else. He ran his hands over the smooth stock, scraped his thumbnail across the ridged frizzen plate, and then he fitted the slight curve of the butt against his shoulder. It was his gun no matter who paid for it.

They splashed among the button bushes, picking up their possessions from the water. "I reckon the powder's wet," said Tobe in disgust, as he held up the dripping wallet.

"Oh, I think likely not," replied Mr. Twistletree. "Once before, I went into a river and wet my powder and missed shooting a little creamy-yellow buffalo bull. And since that time I've carried it in a leather poke with the inside coated twice with beeswax. It keeps out the damp very handily."

Tobe grinned. Old Twistletree had a head on him after all. He'd heard of folks doing such a trick, but he never before knew anybody who'd actually taken all that trouble to do it. He splashed around and found most of their things, even his powder horn. Only his shotpouch, filled with newly molded lead balls, was nowhere to be found.

"Likely that scoundrel took it," Tobe told himself. "I hope his rifle barrel gets full of mud and busts open in his face when he tries to fire my bullets."

He gathered up his clothes, the blankets, and the skillet and set out toward camp. Mr. Twistletree followed him along the twisting riverbank, shaking water from his bird skins and talking about how the feathers were losing their color and they wouldn't be worth showing in Philadelphia. Tobe hardly heard. He was busy planning some way to earn four silver shillings and pay back Mr. Twistletree.

He glanced over his shoulder after a spell, for he didn't want his master wandering away, looking for some beetle, with the sun going down and camp to make and all these things to dry. Mr. Twistletree was standing by a sycamore tree with his head cocked on one side. "Hark now," he said softly. "Ain't that a turkey I hear?"

Tobe listened and heard faintly a gobbler's weird call.

"A young one, I'll be bound," Mr. Twistletree

went on. "An old bird's voice is sweeter and not so coarse. Perhaps we can summon it here to our pot, boy. Make haste!"

Tobe flung down his gear and scurried into the bushes behind the man. With trembling fingers he wiped out the pan with the sleeve of the great coat. He tore off a piece of tow cloth and ran it back and forth in the barrel to get out the dampness. Taking the powder wallet, he managed to get a handful down the barrel.

But what was the use of it? He didn't have any lead shot. He turned to tell Mr. Twistletree and found the man holding out a handful of small buckshot, the kind he used in his fowling piece.

"Maybe if you use four or five of them," he whispered, "it'll do for turkey at close range."

Tobe took them and settled down to wait. Mr. Twistletree got down on his knees and picked a small green leaf. He placed it some way in his cupped fingers. Suddenly, stretching his scrawny neck, he put his hands to his mouth and gobbled.

Tobe all but dropped his gun. He stared in amazement. It would be a great temptation to shoot anything that sounded that much like a turkey. And a body might get Mr. Twistletree half plucked before he discovered his mistake, he thought, almost laughing to himself.

Still and all, it was a fine and useful talent to have. Every time Mr. Twistletree gobbled, the turkey answered, coming closer and closer.

They were well hidden in the cluster of calico bushes and little young hornbeam trees. Tobe tensed slightly, for the turkey was near now. He peered out through the branches sharply. Mr. Twistletree began to gobble again.

And suddenly there was a flash of tawny yellow fur. Tobe saw glaring eyes and outstretched claws right in his face and a great weight crashed into him. It was the biggest catamount he'd ever seen in his life!

Five

The huge cat sent Tobe sprawling backwards. He clutched out to save himself, knocking his rifle against a sapling. It went off with a roar, and he heard Mr. Twistletree scream. Tobe's arm twisted under him somehow, sending a sharp pain across his shoulders.

The painter snarled and the bushes lashed about. Tobe didn't know what was happening, for he couldn't get himself untangled from the great coat and the bushes, with his arm bent beneath him. At last he floundered up out of the coat, half-naked.

The cat critter was gone, but Mr. Twistletree lay on the ground, twitching and shuddering like a bird with a broken neck. There was blood everywhere and he kept making the most awful gasping, choking noises.

Horrified, Tobe pulled the coat over his shoulders and scrambled over to the man. The painter must have chewed out his vitals or bitten him in the gullet, the way he was taking on. With stiff hands Tobe turned him over. Mr. Twistletree, with his mouth wide open and blood streaming from the side of his head, went right on making his terrible sounds.

"What ails you?" gasped Tobe. "Be you dying?"

Mr. Twistletree tried to sit up, but he couldn't. He rolled over on his side, shaking and strangling. "He's going fast," thought Tobe, and he didn't know what he ought to do. He halfway stood up, thinking he'd get the skillet and fetch some water.

But Mr. Twistletree looked up then and lifted his hand. "Not hurt," he gasped. "Oh, my body and soul!" He doubled up and clutched his side.

"Laughing!" cried Tobe. "You're laughing! What ails you anyhow? What's there to laugh at?"

What was so funny about being slapped around by a catamount and getting all scratched up? Why, they could have both been killed right out. He squatted to stare at the man.

But the more he thought about it, the funnier it became. He remembered how he'd thought it would be easy to take Mr. Twistletree for a turkey, and that's what the painter had gone and done. It had come creeping, creeping ever so softly through the forest with its mouth watering and its claws twitching for a fine fat turkey, very sure of itself, because painters didn't mistake men for turkeys ever.

Then it had leaped through the bushes into their hiding place and what had it found? A skinny man in spectacles and a three-cornered hat!

"That painter must have felt a proper fool,"

thought Tobe, and he began to laugh too. The more he laughed, the funnier it seemed and he and Asa Twistletree together rocked and chuckled among the calico bushes.

Mr. Twistletree grew quieter and wiped his eyes. "Oh, there we were, the tiger and I," he said. "Both of us expecting to see the handsome bird. Which was more surprised—I to see the big cat or he to see the gobbling human?"

His shoulders shook as he began to laugh again. "He was chagrined right down to his whiskers to see us," he cried. "Right in the middle of his leap he tried to turn aside, to right this awful blunder. But it was too late! He'd been fooled to a fare-thee-well. Oh, oh, oh!"

He fell back laughing once more, but Tobe stood up. "You been hurt," he pointed out. "You're bleeding bad."

Mr. Twistletree sat up and touched his temple. "Only a scratch," he said. "Nothing to be concerned over. But, Tobias, we've lost our supper. And what's more I've lost my spectacles and cannot get about without them."

Tobe searched around among the leaves. He had almost given up hope of finding the spectacles when he saw them hanging in a bush. The frame was bent, and one eyeglass was shattered.

"They're broke," he said sadly, handing them over.

The man sighed. "Ah, well, I've another pair.

But this day's work has been costly; I won't deny it." He squinted around at Tobe and grinned. "But then it ain't often a man can get the better of a hunting beast, the way we did." He chuckled.

Tobe nodded his head. That was true, for a fact. It was a thing to remember and tell about all his life, how the two of them had made a painter act the fool. He felt almost friendly toward Asa Twistletree. Two bodies could hardly laugh so long and so loud together and not be friends.

And he was sorry about the day costing such a heap of money. The cost of the spectacles couldn't be helped. But it was money thrown away to buy a rifle that already belonged to you. It was wicked to pay a thief for stolen goods.

"You shouldn't have give that man money for my rifle." He said it straight out.

"Why not?" asked Mr. Twistletree. "We had to have your rifle or we couldn't go on. There was nothing to stop the man from taking it. He didn't have to sell it. He could have shot us both and taken the rifle and the money." He gave the boy a wry look. "Neither you nor I could have defended ourselves against him."

Tobe looked away. Mr. Twistletree's face grew troubled. "I'm sorry if you think I behaved in a cowardly or otherwise disreputable fashion, Tobias," he declared. "But I have found that I have no weapons but my wits. I must use them the best way I can."

He straightened out his spectacles and put them on. With one eye closed he got to his feet, went back to the spot where they had dropped their possessions, and began to pick up the blankets and skillet.

Tobe stepped forward to help. He gathered up the rest of the things and they made their way back to where the horse grazed. The fire had long since died. But Tobe spotted a dead pine, and before dark he had it down and wood enough stacked up for the nightlong fire, though it hadn't been easy, working in the loose coat.

He was weak as branch water when he finished, and he wasn't looking forward to going to bed empty again. But at least he'd sleep warm and dry. He hung his wet clothes by the fire and Mr. Twistletree's blanket too. The man hadn't given it a thought and was stumbling around in the twilight looking for heaven knows what.

Tobe had no more than sat down close to the blaze when Mr. Twistletree handed him something sliced up on a pine chip. It looked queer and twisted and too black to be anything but spoiled. "Whatever's this?" he asked.

"Eat it. It's good," the man urged. "Go on, try a bite."

Tobe cut off the least little bit with his knife and put it on his tongue. He began to chew it cautiously. But it was good, he found. It was tasty, almost like meat.

"Whatever is it?" he asked again, taking a whole slice this time.

"It's puffball," replied Mr. Twistletree.

"Puffball!" Tobe spat his mouthful into the fire. "Them's poison! It's sure death to eat puffball."

"No, it ain't," answered Mr. Twistletree, popping a piece into his mouth. "I've eaten many a one. And I'd hardly be killing you, nor me, if I could help it."

He began to take tree buds and sticks and bark and a crinkly root out of his pockets and dumped them into the skillet of water he'd set over the fire to boil. "And I'll have some hot tea in a moment," he explained.

Tobe stared at the things on the pine shingle. Whoever heard tell of folks eating such truck? But it did taste good. And he was powerful hungry. He was ashamed when he realized that he'd eaten almost all the puffballs and Mr. Twistletree had hardly had one. He drank the queer-tasting tea too. It was hot and filling and perked him up considerable. By the time he'd gotten back into his own dry clothes, he was feeling almost his old self again.

But he was too sleepy to sit up any longer. The minute his blanket was dry, he went to bed and was asleep before he'd pulled the cover over his head.

He woke once in the night. It was black as a crow's wing. The fire was just winking. He felt chilly, and his legs ached like they were about to drop clean off. His blanket must not have been all the way dry, for it lay damp and heavy and cold over his knees. He wished suddenly he was home. A body that slept in a shuck mattress with a little sister and two brothers had small chance of getting cold or lonely. And his mam would never have sent him to bed with any such strange meal as that he'd had this night.

Mr. Twistletree stirred and got up. Tobe could hear him stumbling over to the firewood in the dark. The man groaned a little as he bent over for the logs. A moment later the pine was on the fire and blazing up, and its warmth jumped out at Tobe. With his blanket he scooted a little nearer.

"Be you awake, lad?" asked Mr. Twistletree. "Are you feverish?"

"Naw," answered Tobe. "I'm fine," and added softly, "thank ye kindly."

The man went back to his blanket with a sigh.

Tobe stared at the fire. Mr. Twistletree was a good man, better than Tobe had ever thought he could turn out to be. He didn't reckon anybody would choose to be skinny and twisty-faced and half-blind and foolish-looking, if he had the choice. But who got to choose such things?

The little flames leaped up and down. Tobe couldn't for the life of him understand a body who spent the day studying ants or skinning little thimble-sized birds he never meant to eat. But Tobe wished he hadn't acted so short and sullen these last few days. Mr. Twistletree might be flighty-headed, but he had a good heart in spite of that. Look how he had fixed the supper, and now he had worried over Tobe in the night.

And after all, Mr. Twistletree—for all his book learning—knew a heap about things, like about puffballs not killing folks and how to keep powder dry and calling up turkeys. And he'd got Tobe's rifle back the only way he knew how and risked his neck to do it too. It was true that as soon as that woodsy found out Mr. Twistletree had money, he could have killed him and had the money and rifle to boot.

Tobe grinned a little and stretched out his hand and touched his rifle. Tomorrow, as soon as he had molded some more bullets for his rifle, he'd have to shoot a deer. He'd gone hungry long enough. And then he slept again.

Six

For almost a week the man and the boy wandered along with the Tennessee River on one side and a mountain in the distance on the other. Oaks were tasseling and opening out leaves as small and pink as a baby's hand. Poplar trees and beeches leafed out in new green; faded redbud flowers littered the ground. Under the haze of gold and green the creamy dogwood floated. It was enough to make a body jump, coming on such ghostly-looking trees in the twilight, Tobe thought.

It was a queer thing to be roaming the woods, carefree as he'd never been before and yet not free at all. In the clearings deer nibbled at tender new grasses, bears on creeks slapped at spawning fish, turkeys sat half-hidden on their purple-speckled eggs.

Tobe's finger twitched on his rifle trigger. He was trying hard not to show how he felt. He'd made up his mind to do what Mr. Twistletree wanted from now on and not worry with anything else.

After all, it wasn't but six months, like his mam had told him.

When he first came out with the man, Tobe had pondered for a spell on running away. But he never would have. He'd given his word to serve this time, and he'd do it. Besides, it would be the same as murder to leave Mr. Twistletree alone in the woods, especially now they'd lost the fowling piece.

Tobe had seen bound-out boys before this who'd got a heap worse bargain than he had—boys whose masters beat them or starved them or worked them like poor dumb critters. And here he was, out in the woods with mighty little to do and most generally enough to eat. And when he went hungry, he couldn't rightfully blame Mr. Twistletree for the lack of game.

The naturalist stopped by a fallen tree. Tobe, right behind him, sighed. Every single time they came to a down tree, it meant an hour's wait while Mr. Twistletree sniffed around it like a bear cub after a bees' nest.

Mr. Twistletree frowned. He'd heard that sigh. "I'm sorry you find your employment so tedious, boy," he said and his voice rasped. He turned back to the log and ran his finger under a piece of bark.

Tobe bit his lip. He hadn't meant to seem unmannerly. But somehow things got crossways between the two of them, no matter what.

Mr. Twistletree stripped back the bark and leaned over the naked wood to peer at whatever might have been uncovered. Tobe, to make up for the sigh, peered too. A power of crawly things scurried off from the light, the way it always happened if you pulled bark off a down tree.

"Whoeeee!" Tobe cried. "Look at them slugs! Big as my thumb!"

He touched one of the big glistening creatures, and its horns sank down out of sight in its head. A great orange and black varmint with nearabout a thousand legs uncurled and twisted away. And that was about all there was that Tobe could see.

Mr. Twistletree muttered to himself as he edged along the trunk. Turning, he said suddenly, "These are the little beasts which have caught my fancy." He pointed to some tiny dull brown beetles trundling up the log. "There are many of them about. I never fail to find them under the bark of certain kinds of trees. I am trying to discover what they eat."

"Well, they ain't got much choice," said Tobe with a grin. "Them slugs look like they're pretty tough."

The man frowned. "I don't know," he said slowly. "It may be they eat wood. At any rate they burrow through it. See these little tunnels, going here and there and looping about? These beetles made them. Engraver beetles, I've heard them called because they make this pretty tracing."

Tobe looked closer. "It's mighty fine," he agreed politely. He thought hard, trying to find something else to say about the beetles. "It looks like writing," he burst out finally. "Like what you put in your ledger book! Now ain't that funny? This here little bug can write and I can't."

"Can't you?" Mr. Twistletree asked, and gave him a queer look. He picked up the saddlebag he had dropped at his feet. "Come along, boy. We'll find a place to camp and then you can go hunting."

Tobe stood a moment watching the mare rub against a tree. "That critter's been doing that all day long," he said. "Pretty good sign rain's a-coming." He drew in a breath of warm air and gazed up at the milky sky. "Them clouds are scaring up bad weather. We'd best find us a cave," he went on. "It'll rain tonight and likely tomorrow too."

"Very well." His master nodded. "We'll seek out a bold bluff and den up like the cleverest of foxes."

They found a dry cave in the side of a little rocky hill. It was low and smelled of wolves, but Mr. Twistletree didn't seem to notice the rank mustiness. The horse didn't like it and, even hobbled, it shambled off down the hill, snorting uneasily. Tobe took his rifle and went hunting, glad to get away finally. He left the man spreading out his bird skins at the cave's entrance.

He broke into a run, went hurtling down a slope, sliding, slipping, and leaping wildly from tree root to rock. He waved his arms and shouted till the little hollow below him seemed filled with voices calling to each other. Then he tripped and went rolling down, laughing fit to bust, carrying along with him a mess of leaves and rocks and sticks.

His gun went off, and he didn't even care. Sprawled on his back at the bottom, he lay looking up, panting and grinning to himself. The spring afternoon filled the woods with a soft amber light, and the air was sweet enough to eat with buttered bread.

"Reckon that racket scared off all the game," he said to himself. And hadn't he acted a fool, carrying on like he had a head full of dry leaves and butterflies? But he'd got all the kinks out of himself anyway and felt like Tobias Bledsoe again.

He stood up and loaded his rifle, considering which way to go. At last he made his way up the hollow to a creek and followed it a ways, going softly, for there were deer sign everywhere. He skirted some calico bushes, and there was a young doe drinking.

It stood with its thin strong legs spraddled out and its pretty head bent. Just as he raised his rifle, the animal jerked its head around, its nostrils flaring as it sniffed the air. It was an easy shot. Tobe was almost disappointed. Keen as he was feeling, he felt sure he could have run the creature down and caught it barehanded.

Still he had a heap to do and the rain had already begun. Its light splattering on the leaves closed in around him. He'd get wet finding wood, but he didn't mind. It was going to be mighty fine to sit in a dry cave and eat deer meet and throw the bones outside into the wet. He gutted the deer and cut off most of its neck and head. It was light enough for him to tote, and he headed back with it across his shoulder.

Mr. Twistletree sat counting the feathers in a bird's wing, but he seemed glad to see the deer meat. And when Tobe had the fire going, the man cooked his strip and ate it hungrily. Tobe was too famished to wait for his collops to cook. He had to eat his first three pieces hardly more than warm from the fire.

"I might as well be an Injun, I eat so much raw meat lately," he told himself, wiping his mouth with his sleeve.

He didn't stop at three pieces. He was going to get full for once. And he went right on roasting pieces and gobbling them down till he was full as a tick in a summer cow pasture.

Mr. Twistletree sharpened the point of his pen and then sat by the blaze with his skins around him on the floor in careful rows. Tobe stared out the cave door at the scattered puddles reflecting what little light was left. Rainy weather was fine for sleeping, and he aimed to climb into his blanket soon. If the firewood lasted, they'd be snug in here all day tomorrow, and he could smoke the rest of the deer meat.

There was a dead sapling lying right over there.

He hadn't noticed it before. He might as well get it now before it got too wet. That way he'd be certain-sure to have enough wood for the next day. He ran out with his hatchet and cut the tree into lengths. Hickory, he told himself, pleased. Hickory was fine for smoking meat.

He dropped one of the lengths on the fire and put the rest in a neat stack with the wood he'd cut earlier. He was squatting by the fire, cutting some of the meat into strips, when all at once Mr. Twistletree sprang to his feet, flinging his book to one side.

"A fire dragon, boy!" he yelled shrilly, grabbing at the hickory. "Quick, quick!" He snatched again at the burning wood with his bare hand. Tobe caught up a stick and pushed the log out of the fire.

"A fire dragon," repeated Mr. Twistletree, and there on the smoking bark sat a tiny glistening black and gold creature with its head raised and its little gullet going in and out like the dasher on a butter churn.

Tobe stared at it in bewilderment. Who would have thought the man would yell so and risk getting roasted for a lizard? For a fact, Asa Twistletree was the daftest man that ever lived.

Mr. Twistletree reached down and picked up the beast. He set it on the palm of his hand and touched its head gently with his thumb.

"Behold the fire dragon," he exclaimed. "It lives among the hottest flames unharmed and eats fire for sustenance. Its powers are such that the fiercest Oriental tyrant, the cruelest Pharaoh, might cower before it. Its venom once slew half the armies of Alexander the Great in India. And a coat made of fire-dragon skins might be valued above rubies, for it can shed fire as a duck's feathers shed water."

Tobe looked at the animal solemnly. "I never heared tell lizards were poisonous," he said at last.

Mr. Twistletree put a finger under one of the dragon's front feet and its toes splayed out till it looked for all the world like a human hand.

"Oh, you're right there," he told him. "This salamander isn't poisonous a-tall. He's as harmless as a butterfly."

Tobe came closer. "I've seen fellers like him swimming in creeks," he went on suspiciously. "How come if'n he's so almighty fond of fire, he's always hanging around creeks?"

Mr. Twistletree stooped and put the salamander down on a ledge at the side of the cave. It sat still as a stone for a spell, and then it went easing off through the dust.

"Oh, that's all nonsense about fire," Mr. Twistletree said absently.

"Then how come he was in our fire?" cried Tobe in exasperation. What made this man say all those fool things if they weren't true?

"Why, I guess you put him there, Tobias," answered Mr. Twistletree with a cackle of laughter. "A salamander likes cool places, damp, dark places

—under stones and in mud and under the bark of rotting logs. When you put that last log on the fire, you put him along with it. When his home got over-warm, he came out to escape and found himself trapped by the flames. If I hadn't pulled him out, he would have burned to ashes, the same as any other living creature."

He stooped and picked up his ledger book where he had flung it down. "It was because folks so often saw him in fires that the notion got around that he liked it. But he didn't get there a-purpose."

"Didn't folks never see him get burned up?" asked Tobe.

"Often, I suppose." Mr. Twistletree nodded. "But men find it hard to part with magical beliefs. There was an old Roman writer named Pliny, a natural philosopher like myself. He put a fire dragon in the flames and watched it perish. But he still went right on believing that fire wouldn't harm the creature. He wanted to believe it so much, he denied the evidence of his own eyes."

"Well, he was mighty simple, then," Tobe muttered. "If a body can't believe what he sees, what can he believe?"

Mr. Twistletree sat down again and began to turn the pages of his book. "I've seen some things so queer, they were difficult to believe, very difficult," he said. "And as for changing what men think, that's well-nigh impossible."

His face sagged into its usual sour lines, and he went back to his writing.

Tobe spread out his blanket, thinking about the salamander. He'd love to show one to his sister Tildy and tell her about how folks thought it ate fire and all that other foolishment. Old Twistle-tree knew a heap of things, even if they weren't worth knowing.

He lay down. That old Roman feller—what was his name? Plumy? Well, of course, you couldn't hold him so much to blame. He lived way back yonder before the first settlers came over to America on sailing ships. He'd be bound to be ignorant.

But Tobe couldn't help wondering just before he went to sleep what other things old Plumy had seen that he hadn't been able to believe.

When he woke up, something heavy seemed to press over his face and down into his nose and throat. Choking and gasping, he sat up. The cave was full of smoke, thick and horrible-smelling. All at once the whole wall seemed to explode, and a flame flicked out at Tobe, quick and skin-scorching.

"Mr. Twistletree!" roared Tobe. "Wake up! The cave's on fire!"

Seven

Tobe crouched on hands and knees and peered into the red haze all around him. A thick yellow puff of smoke rose up in his face and went scalding down his throat. He staggered to his feet, gasping and moaning. It must be the end of the world, the very rocks were blazing!

"Mr. Twistletree!" he screamed in panic.

For answer there was only the crackle and hiss of the fire.

There was a sudden roar, and all around him the ropy smoke lit up with a red and evil light. Tobe howled and ran. He stepped on something hard and round, and even in his fear he recognized his precious rifle. Stooping, he grabbed it up and ran on, coughing and choking, until at last he plunged out into the mild spring night.

He took a deep breath of the damp air. It wasn't the end of the world after all, only the cave was afire. But Mr. Twistletree was still in there and the powder. Tobe might as well have left his rifle as leave the powder. He would have to go back.

He dropped his gun and turned around. The
curdled smoke flooded out of the cave. Strange
shadows writhed and twisted in the depths. Tobe
shivered. It wasn't that he was so scared of fire. He'd
been in fires before this, but it wasn't natural for
rocks to blaze up. It might be the devil himself
lived in there.

Still he had to do it, he told himself, and leaped
into the cave. The fire boiled around his knees and
the hot air strangled in his throat. Once he thought

he saw Mr. Twistletree. He tried to call out, but he could only squeak. His gullet felt as if he'd swallowed red-hot embers.

He hadn't the least notion where the powder was. With tears running from his eyes, he dropped to his knees and fumbled over the cave floor. He had almost given up when his hand struck the leather wallet. A little stream of fire, quick as a snake's tongue, ran under his arm as he reached out. He clawed the powder to him and sprang upright.

The wallet was hot to the touch. It would go up in his arms and he would be blown so high, eagles would ask him the time of day. He'd have to get it out and come back a third time for Mr. Twistletree.

He began to run and whammed hard into the wall. He reeled about, dazed, and started off in another direction. The air was as thick and yellow as clabbered cream, and it charred his throat till he couldn't swallow. Flames spouted up in front of him, so close he almost flung down the powder and ran.

He dodged away and stood a moment in confusion. He had to get out. It was certain death to stay here. The wallet seemed to smolder in his arms. He hugged it to his chest as if he could keep the heat away. With one hand before him, he wobbled through the cave and found himself once more out in the open air.

He sprawled flat on the ground, letting the powder fall beside him. He flopped over on his back, and the cool rain slid over his neck and face. He couldn't seem to get enough air into his parched lungs, but after a spell he could breathe evenly again.

He was surprised to find he wasn't the only one who was wheezing and coughing. Mr. Twistletree crouched by his side with his hands held stiffly in front of him.

"I saved my bird skins. Every one of them," he cried. "But I seem to have burnt my hands."

Tobe hardly heard what he said. He was still too dazed and frightened to do more than stare around. Every time a gust of brimstone-filled smoke gushed out of the cave, he winced.

Finally he turned to the naturalist. "How come it to do that?" he asked. "How come solid rock to catch afire like a stubble field?"

The man turned his hands over so the rain fell on his blistered palms. "That was no ordinary rock, that was coal," he answered.

"Coal?" repeated Tobe. "You mean charcoal?"

"No, no," went on Mr. Twistletree. "This is rock coal. Some say it is a kind of petrified wood, but I don't know. At any rate it burns like wood, only hotter and longer."

He fell silent a moment, and Tobe stared at the flames licking out of the smoke.

Mr. Twistletree coughed and spoke again. "It's found in the earth, sometimes right on the surface. And we're not the first to set a bed of it afire accidentally. I saw a whole hill aflame once in western Pennsylvania. A hunter's campfire had set the coal to burning fifteen years before I came there."

Tobe glanced uneasily over his shoulder. "You reckon that fire will spread and burn up everything around here?" he asked, licking his cracked lips.

The naturalist shook his head. "I think not," he said. "We'll be quite safe here, Tobias, if we can find some shelter from the rain."

They stumbled through the dark till they found a suitable place under the bluff. Once, after they were settled, Tobe asked Mr. Twistletree, "Do folks in Philadelphia ever make a fire of coal?"

"There are some who have tried it," replied the philosopher. "But most are afeared of it. They don't understand it and they're not willing to learn."

Tobe could see how it was. Rock coal was fearsome stuff. Besides, with trees in plenty all around, who needed anything else to make a fire out of? And he fell into an uneasy sleep.

Tobe reckoned he'd never spent a less happy night. The cliff didn't provide much shelter from the wet, and as the night wore on, he grew colder and colder, and the rocks under him harder and harder. He kept dreaming about fire and waking up in a tremor. When daylight came at last, he was stiff and aching, his head throbbed queerly, and his eyes burned and stung.

It was raining heavily, and the way the wind blew in little gusts from every side gave Tobe the notion the weather wasn't going to change any time soon. He dragged himself up and went off to have a look at the cave. The fire was still burning down in the earth, for wisps and puffs of the stinking smoke rose up from the split in the floor at times.

It looked safe enough and he went in. He could breathe without choking, for most of the smoke was gone. The rock was hot under his feet and his clothes steamed in the warm dry air.

The three-legged skillet would never be any good again. The heat had cracked it in two. And the great coat was gone. Tobe turned over the little heap of burnt rags that was left, and one of the bone buttons shivered to powder under his fingers.

Part of the meat he'd been smoking was charred into black strings, not fit food for skunks, who'd eat anything. He was glad now he hadn't brought it all inside the cave. The haunch and back strips that were left would feed them for several days.

To one side he saw his blanket. A corner was darkly scorched and there were a few holes in it, but it was still plenty good. And his knife and tomahawk lying beside it hadn't been harmed a lick. He whooped when he saw them. He'd figured on having to make an Injun ax with a sharp stone and a stick.

Tobe gathered up his possessions and glanced around. Whatever Mr. Twistletree had left here had been burned to ashes. But he reckoned his master hadn't left anything behind that he valued.

"He'd of stayed here and been roasted like a collop of meat before he'd of left any of them skins or that old ledger book," he said with a grin, as he tramped through the rain back to their camp.

"Only you wouldn't name it a camp," he thought, staring down at the bird skins and Asa Twistletree sleeping away while the wet trickled down his face.

Tobe worked hard at getting a fire going, and with the damp and his sore muscles it took quite a while. But he had the meat cooking by the time the naturalist woke. Mr. Twistletree stared blearily at Tobe, then got up and walked stiff-legged to the fire. His hands were red and there were blisters on the backs of them, Tobe could see.

"Well, Tobias, we've come through fire and flood," the man rasped out. "And I'm pleased to see you have staved off famine for the present."

Tobe grinned. "It ain't much but it'll feed us while we hole up here for a spell," he said. "You nor me neither is fit to travel, and the weather ain't fixing to change for two, three days."

Mr. Twistletree chewed his meat and looked mournfully at his hands. "Whatever you say, boy," he answered. "My hands are painful and my head is filled with smoke, and were today the brightest and balmiest of the year, I fear me I could not stir away from this spot."

Tobe worked the livelong day, in spite of his aching head and his soreness. He built a half-faced shelter of hemlock boughs and slabs of elm bark. The open side faced the fire and the cliff wall, and he was proud of it and of how warm and dry it was. He cut a heaping plenty of wood and piled it by the fire.

Mr. Twistletree was no help. He just sat with mud poultices on his blisters and with his hands thrust out in front of him like birds spitted on canes.

The next day the rain was coming down harder than ever, and there wasn't a frazzling thing to do. Tobe wished he hadn't finished all the work yesterday, for he was feeling mighty fine after his night's rest and he hated to sit idle. He figured once he'd go out and hunt down the mare, but there was no telling how much longer the rain would last. And he reckoned there was little point in fetching the beast till they needed it.

Mr. Twistletree read, since his hands were still too stiff to write. He had a little fat book of some sort, and he sat by the fire turning the pages, one after the other, while Tobe moved restlessly around, feeling cramped and uneasy. A hundred times he peered outside, hoping for a sign the weather was going to change.

"One thing about old Twistletree," he thought. "As long as he's got them bird skins and them books, he don't seem to mind where he's at or what's happened to him."

The time dragged by. The rain dripped into puddles, and the fire chattered quietly to itself. Tobe yawned tremendously. Finally he crawled out of the shelter and sat with his back against the cliff and his head resting against the rock. He stared up at the wet trees, shifting about, trying to see the top of a tall poplar. Something crunched between his skull and the stone. He turned to see what it could be.

It was a dirt dobber's nest, little mud pipes stuck fast to the rock. Tobe brushed the dried mud from his hair and shoulders. A couple of spiders, frail and dry, fell to his leg.

"Wonder how come dirt dobbers build them things just for spiders to hatch out of?" he asked himself. It was mighty thoughty of the dirt dobbers, but now that he came to think of it, it was a plumb queer thing to do. He'd ask Mr. Twistletree. His master knew so all-fired much, let him try to answer this. Let him and old Plumy both figure on it.

"Mr. Twistletree," he said aloud.

The naturalist looked up, but Tobe could see he wasn't rightly paying attention. It was a funny thing. Mr. Twistletree could get so deep in his study, he couldn't seem to hear, and yet he did hear too.

Once when Tobe had asked a question and he could tell by the way Mr. Twistletree answered that he didn't rightly know what Tobe was saying, Tobe had asked, "How come your hair don't grow but on one side of your head?"

Mr. Twistletree had smiled faintly and gone back to his writing with a shake of his head. But the very next day he had turned to Tobe and asked, "Is there something the matter with my hair? Doesn't it grow the same as other folks?"

Tobe had been mighty put out and stammered and turned red. But he'd learned not to put any faith in Mr. Twistletree's not hearing him.

"Mr. Twistletree!" he repeated now, and the man blinked and put down his book to let Tobe know that this time he was really paying some mind. "How come dirt dobbers to build these here mud things for spiders to hatch out of?" inquired Tobe.

The naturalist rubbed his chin with his knuckles. "Is that what they do? Are you certain?"

"Why, I never broke one of them mud things in my life didn't spiders come out," Tobe told him triumphantly. "Just like this one here now."

"Little new young spiders?" asked the philosopher.

"Well, naw," Tobe answered. "These here dried-up ones is the onliest ones a body ever finds inside."

"Maybe some day I can show you a spider's silky egg when the young ones hatch, Tobias," said Mr. Twistletree. "Out comes a whole mist of such frail little bodies, the slightest breath can send them hurtling into space. No, the dirt dobber nest is built for her own young ones. And she's clever enough to seal a few spiders in the mud to be food for her nestlings when they hatch."

Tobe's mouth dropped open. Why, it wasn't so. Tobe's own pappy had always told him spiders hatched out of the dirt dobber's mud nest. All the folks on the Holston knew it for a fact. It was one of those things everybody had always known. They might not know why it was so, but they knew it *was* so.

Tobe shut his mouth slowly. Still, he had to admit that he'd never seen any kind of spiders but dead ones in these dirt houses. He poked at the nest and broke open another little room. Two more spider skins floated down. He didn't want to be like old Plumy, disbelieving his own eyes.

It might be that Mr. Twistletree was right. He'd sure spent enough time watching such varmints to know. But it wasn't likely that the old mammy dirt dobber would work out a fancy scheme like Mr. Twistletree said. Then again why should she go to such a heap of trouble for spiders? Tobe pressed his lips together, not sure what to think.

"Did old Plumy know about this?" he asked at last.

Mr. Twistletree looked puzzled. "Plumy? Oh, Pliny," he exclaimed. "Perhaps he did. He knew a lot of things. Now wait." He rummaged in his saddlebag and drew out another book. "Here are some of Pliny's writings. Make yourself comfortable, boy, and I'll read it to you."

The wind rose, swelling and roaring in the hemlocks, whistling along under the cliff to make the fire leap about like a live thing. The rain swept over the shelter. Above it all, Mr. Twistletree rasped on, and Tobe settled down to think about deer hunting. But something caught his ear, and the next thing he knew he was listening for all he was worth.

Oh, it was queer that an old fellow living so long ago could know such a heap of different things! Some of the things Tobe found hardest to believe, like flying fish, Mr. Twistletree said were true. Wouldn't that be something to see—a fish skimming along over the Holston River like a swallow?

Then again, some things that seemed likely enough, like unicorns, weren't true at all. If a beast could have two horns, it stood to reason some beast could have only one in the middle of its forehead.

The fire had almost died before Mr. Twistletree stopped reading. Tobe got up and put more wood on the blaze and poked it up a mite. "I reckon there's just a heap more things in this world than most folks know about," he said slowly.

The naturalist didn't answer. Tobe glanced down at the book lying open on the blanket. He didn't know whether it was upside down or not. And then he caught sight of great A that his granny had taught him out of the Bible when he was a little chap up in Kentuck. He sort of wished he knew more of his letters. It might be handy to know how to read some time.

He looked up and saw Mr. Twistletree watching him. Tobe turned quickly away. "We best eat," he said gruffly.

The next day came up windy and bright. Tobe

was mighty glad to fetch up the horse and load their few belongings on it. It would be a good day for traveling. The air was fresh smelling, and not far off a puddle full of frogs purred and creaked. A sweet shrub opened its dark red flowers, fringed like a hunting shirt, close by the cliff. Tobe broke off a twig and smelled the blossom, then stuck it in the horse's tangled mane.

Tobe helped the naturalist to mount. "This ain't the way to travel, a fine day like this," grumbled Mr. Twistletree. "But my knees are stiff and my hands not yet healed. So I'll ride, for I'm anxious to get on south."

The boy frowned. "South?" he asked. "I figured we'd be turning back."

The naturalist looked down at him. "Nay, why should we turn back, boy? You're bound till September and we'll be back to the Holston settlements in ample time."

Tobe reddened. "I ain't studying on my binding time," he told the man angrily. "But this here's Injun country. And the spring of the year ain't no time to be snooping around in Chickamauga territory."

Mr. Twistletree looked startled. "I thought these were Cherokee Indians," he said slowly. "I thought they were all kindly disposed toward white men."

Tobe grinned, a little cruelly. There were things aplenty old Twistletree didn't know, nor Pliny either. And this was sure one of them.

"There's some Cherokees that ain't friends of white men and never will be till they die," the boy answered. "Folks call them Chickamaugas, for they left the Cherokee nation and went to live by themselves along Chickamauga Creek. They're mean as Beelzebub himself. Ain't you heared tell of the killing they done at Nashville and how they burn folks they catch flatboating down the river?"

The naturalist looked worried. "I didn't know," he said at last. He pondered, cleaning his spectacles on his sleeve. "Well, I have no choice. My journey was paid for me by a man in Philadelphia on condition that I visit an ancient fortification. Here."

Mr. Twistletree showed Tobe a piece of paper roughly marked with lines and letters. "This is a map he obtained from a Cherokee chief, and there's the fortification, right there. I must find it for I am greatly in this man's debt. It wouldn't be right not to fulfill his wishes, if I can."

He sighed. "I would leave you here to wait for me, Tobias, and go on alone. But we have only one gun. Take you or leave you, I risk your life."

Tobe stared. They could turn back, couldn't they? They were both risking their lives for a piece of foolishness. And how come this Philadelphy feller didn't come down here and see this thing for himself? He must be crazy to pay good money to have somebody else do it for him.

But Tobe could see how it was for Mr. Twistletree. A body wouldn't want to accept a man's money and then not do what he was paid for.

The naturalist spoke to the horse and rode slowly off. "We'll put our faith in Providence," he told the boy. "It may be we'll avoid the Indians altogether. And if we don't, then we must trust that they will see that our errand is innocent and do us no harm as we certainly intend them none."

Tobe shouldered the rifle. "I wisht I had me two or three more of these to put my faith in," he thought. "Mr. Twistletree maybe don't know enough to be scared of Chickamaugas. But I know aplenty. And I'm scared enough right now for him and me both!"

Eight

Day after day they traveled deeper into Chicka-mauga country. They followed the winding trail south till Tobe was sure that every bend would bring them face to face with Chief Dragging Canoe himself or smack in the middle of a war party.

"Look!" cried Mr. Twistletree.

Tobe jumped a foot and readied his rifle for the savage crouching behind the bush.

"What an enormous spicebush!" said the natural-ist and walked on.

Tobe, trembling all over, came after him.

"Hark!" whispered Mr. Twistletree.

Tobe froze in his tracks, listening for all his worth. From the little hill ahead the cry sounded out again. It was the savages signaling to one an-other, using a rain crow's call. But he could tell that was no bird. A human throat made that noise. Then close by a rattling cry answered. Oh, they were surrounded, no mistake. His blood pounded up inside his head till he couldn't think.

"There!" said Asa Twistletree, pointing. "A tree frog making all that noise."

Tobe could have kicked him. He'd made sure it was the Indians this time. He jerked angrily on the mare's rope and trailed off after the naturalist.

The very next afternoon Tobe found moccasin prints in the mud all around a spring, just a whole heap of them. It didn't take him more than a glance to tell they were fresh tracks. The savages were close by this time, so close Tobe made sure he could smell them.

He tried not to get rattled. "We got a chance so long as I keep my head," he told himself. "We can trick them, I figure." He took a deep breath and went back to the trail to hunt for his master.

"Listen," he said, pulling the man out of the bushes. "We ain't the onliest ones using this path. Them Chickamaugas been here not half a day before us."

Tobe was glad to see Mr. Twistletree give a start and look off over his shoulder. He needed scaring if ever a body did.

"I got a plan," Tobe went on. "We'll build a campfire right here and make our supper. Then we'll leave it burning and sneak off and sleep a long ways from the fire, see? And when the Injuns come up, there won't be nary a soul here."

The naturalist was pleased. He beamed at the boy. "A very fine sham," he said.

Tobe built the fire and they cooked their meat

quick. He slung their possessions back on the mare and said, "Let's go."

But the man wouldn't go. "I'm sure the Indians won't come," he told Tobe. "And here are some beetles burying a dead mouse. If I can watch but an hour more, they will have buried it entirely."

Tobe ground his teeth together. "A body like Mr. Twistletree can't rightly help not having good sense," he told himself. "I got to look after him the best I can. But in reason I never knowed anybody who could make it so hard to do."

Mr. Twistletree didn't budge one whit. He lay on the ground with his head propped up on his hand.

Tobe hid the horse and sat right there by Mr. Twistletree with his gun across his lap. But as twilight came on, he got so wearied listening for Indians and straining his eyes for a glimpse of a redskin among the bushes, he went to sleep. Next morning the mouse was gone and Mr. Twistletree was lying in a crumpled heap on the ground, snoring busily.

And when the man woke, did he look to see if he'd been scalped during the night? No! First off he looked for any sign of that mouse.

"He don't mean to risk his life," Tobe thought. "It's just he thinks so much about flowers and trees, he ain't got room in his head for Injuns."

One thing fretted Tobe a heap. If he was to get killed, it would be mortal hard on his mam and Tildy. Betsy and the others would get along all right, no matter what happened, no matter what wild mix-up his pa might get them in. But his mam needed him a heap. He'd always been the one to shoulder the burdens that his father never bothered to pick up. And Tildy—well, Tildy was flighty-headed. She needed him to look after her. She was forever doing things like taking a wager she could hold a bee in her mouth.

So there were good reasons aplenty why he wanted to get Tobias Bledsoe back to the Holston settlements alive and kicking. And he meant to do it.

The trouble was, one body couldn't go on being scared for two, not every single minute he couldn't. And this morning Tobe himself found it hard to keep his mind on Indians and their hatefulness with the light coming down greeny-gold through the new leaves and warming him, when the May apples and blue dogbane made pools all around their camp, and the smell of spring was so sweet and thick in the air, you might almost reach out a hand and touch it. Every breeze shook a yellow snow down on them from the tasseling oaks and hickories.

And it didn't help that old Twistletree wouldn't stay scared. Oh, it had been easy enough for Tobe to make the man tremble sometimes, talking about what happened to travelers the Chickamaugas found on their land. Then the naturalist would promise to walk softly, to keep an eye out for Indian sign, not to do anything foolish.

But right away he'd see a bird he didn't know and

go crashing through the bushes and shoot it for its silly little skin. And how many times had he found a plant and needs must stop right there and dig it up, in plain sight of the trail, in spite of everything Tobe could say.

Now Mr. Twistletree, having poked around in the dirt after his mouse, got to his feet. "Well, boy, let's be on our way," he squeaked. "The chariot of Apollo races on apace and no man may stay its swiftness."

Tobe grinned as he rose. He'd got used to Asa Twistletree talking this foolish way. It came of being a schoolmaster in the wintertime and knowing all about Greek and Latin and such bookish truck as that.

In a few days they walked out of April and into a May filled with silverbells and fire cherry and locust and bush honeysuckle. And not another sign of the redskins did they find.

Tobe began to feel a little easier. Maybe his master was right. Maybe they were going to miss the Chickamaugas altogether. Only sometimes, waking up at night, he'd go cold all over. What sound had roused him? And he'd lie there in the dark thinking how far they were from the Holston River and any sort of help. And some nights it would be all he could do not to get up and go running back the way they'd come.

"It ain't so much further now," announced Mr. Twistletree cheerfully one morning.

Tobe reckoned he was just saying that to encourage him. He could tell the way the man angled the map this way and that, he didn't really know. Tobe didn't say a thing, just followed his master around a big beech that had fallen across the trail. The sky was blue as a bluebird's back, the gnarled crabapple trees made a pink haze in every hollow, and the sun was warm as a friendly hand.

There was a quick flash of scarlet between two hackberry trees. "Yonder's one of them sandhill redbirds," Tobe hollered out.

"Aye," Mr. Twistletree answered, stopping. "And there sits his neat wife with him."

Tobe stopped too and looked up. "I don't see but one," he said finally.

"Why, there she sits, right below him," cried Mr. Twistletree. "She's very still and she's almost the same color as the leaves—there! She flew!"

"You mean that bright red feller has got a wife that ain't even red at all—just green like that?" Tobe asked. "It looks like she'd be anyways pink, don't it?"

But his master had spied a land turtle and gone off to offer it a leaf to eat.

Tobe believed him, however. He believed most nigh everything Mr. Twistletree had told him, since the other day when they'd seen the spider's egg open and all those million little new spiders, no bigger than a fly's eye, go sailing off into the breeze. That had settled the dirt dobber for once and all with Tobe.

Tobe had acted the empty-head, for a fact, that day. He hated to think back to how he'd stood right on the Indian trail with his eyes on the spiders, his rifle propped against a tree and out of quick reach. Why, a whole tribe of Indians could have come up behind him and he would never have known, while he watched the little creatures spin out their faint threads and float off into the sunlight, as brave as if they'd had wild cat claws and bear teeth.

Tobe worried some about his rash actions. Folks that behaved so foolishly as that got laughed at by white men and scalped by red ones. And if Mrs. Haymore had seen him, she'd have poured scalding water on him, too.

Still a body couldn't help noticing things like baby spiders, once he'd had them pointed out to him. It was like letters. Thinking about great A in old Pliny's book had made him see the letter everywhere—where two trees leaned together with a branch between, where a twig lay fallen across two other twigs. He'd showed the trees to Mr. Twistletree, and the man had pointed out how two loops of grapevine sticking out from a sapling made a B.

It was a marvel how many B's Tobe began to see here and yon. Now he knew almost all his letters, and in the evenings, waiting for the meat to cook, he practiced writing in the dirt with a stick. And scarce as paper was, Mr. Twistletree had promised to let him make his letters on a ledger page with the quill pen and to keep that page for his very own.

Tobe knew his mam would be proud as a strutting turkey rooster at what he'd learned.

But his pap would be outdone. He'd think it a waste of time.

"Well, I've naught else to do with time but waste it here in the woods," Tobe reckoned. "And I figure there's times when reading and writing must come in handy, else folks wouldn't take the trouble to learn to do it at all."

May was waning fast and still they journeyed on. Often they covered a good distance from sunup till sundown, but other times they stayed put for days on end while Mr. Twistletree dried roots and leaves to take back with him. The trail finally led over the mountains, and it slowed them down considerable.

The old mare did fine on level ground, but climbing seemed to trouble her wind, and when the way got steep, she heaved so, Tobe was feared she would die. It took all one day and the best part of the next morning to get on top of the mountain.

While the horse got her breath and Mr. Twistletree made a drawing of a toadstool, Tobe went on ahead. He'd made up his mind to shoot a deer if he saw one. It took all his courage to shoot game in Indian country. Firing a rifle was like yelling, "Here we be, come get us."

But up here in the hills it seemed as though they'd left the redskins behind. Tobe didn't even have Indians on his mind at all when he stepped in among those big rocks—and saw the campfire.

A snaky thin wisp of smoke rose up from it. The strength ran out of Tobe's legs the way water runs out of a leaky piggin. Numb with fear, he must have stood staring for a good spell, for he heard Mr. Twistletree and the mare come up behind him.

"Tobias," spoke the man sharply.

Tobe didn't turn. "Looky here," he said in a flat voice. "A campfire. And yonder on that rock . . . they . . . they done mixed war paint on that rock!"

Mr. Twistletree grasped him by the shoulder. "How long have they been gone?" he asked.

Tobe stepped forward then and kicked at the smoldering wood. When it broke open, sparks flew everywhere and the smoke thickened and twisted in the cool bright air.

"Not more than three hours, I reckon," he answered.

Mr. Twistletree's breath whistled sharply in his throat. "Could they be around close?" he inquired in a croaky whisper.

Tobe's eyes slid around. "I reckon they could," he said dully. Behind that rock over there or that sycamore, down in that clump of arrowwood, lying behind that bunch of witch hobble. They could be anywhere, staring out at the man and the boy they meant to kill.

Tobe gave a shiver. "What's that?" he gasped.

Somebody was coming. Some Chickamauga warrior was walking lightly over the dry leaves, not making a lot of noise, but not caring if he was discovered either, and coming closer and closer.

Tobe swung around, his rifle cocked and to his shoulder. He aimed to get in the first shot. After that it didn't matter; they were good as captured.

Who would have thought a 'possum could scuff up the leaves so like a man's footsteps? Who would have thought to see the varmint come walking so grandly out of the woods? And then it stopped and chose a few leaves from those on the ground. With its paws it pushed the leaves back under its belly. Its skinny tail came snaking up and grabbed the bunch, wrapping around them like a cord. The 'possum trotted off, holding its little bundle straight out behind it and grinning to itself.

"If'n he laughs, I'll whop him up side the skull," Tobe thought. "If'n he so much as smiles, I'll wham him hard."

But Mr. Twistletree didn't laugh. Instead he sat down heavily on a rock and swallowed once or twice as though his throat was dry. "I . . . I thought it was an Indian warrior," he rasped out at last. "And it might very well have been. Tobias, I shouldn't have brought you here. I'm not able to look after you well enough in time of danger."

Tobe lowered his rifle. He grinned to himself. "Look after him." Not likely. He was the one to look after old Twistletree, not the other way around. He kicked out at the ashes of the fire.

"Oh, I misdoubt these fellers know we're around," he said easily. "They been gone toward Nashville a good spell, I reckon. There ain't no need to fault yourself, unless you think that was an Injun dressed up like a 'possum to spy on us."

"Oh," said Mr. Twistletree. He stood up and looked relieved. "If you say so, Tobias. You are a level-headed creature."

Tobe didn't answer, but the smile left his face. Once he'd been level-headed, but not any more. Why ever had seeing the 'possum made him think they were safe, he groaned to himself? Oh, being addleheaded must be catching, like the measles. Only a bony-pate like him, or Mr. Twistletree, would think these Injuns had gone on to Nashville, when there, sticking out from behind a rock, plain as day, was a brown bare leg, striped and streaked with red war paint!

Nine

Tobe wanted to run. More than anything he wanted to light out through the rocks and trees and get far away from here. Nobody would blame him that he left Mr. Twistletree behind. A growed man ought not to come dragging his bound boy into Indian territory.

But there was no use thinking about it. He just couldn't sell out and leave old Twistletree to face the Chickamaugas all alone. He didn't know why, but he couldn't.

And anyway, he was too scared to run. It was more than he could do to lift a foot. He couldn't even reach out a hand to stop the nag when she trotted suddenly by him and walked right over the Indian. Her hoof struck the warrior's leg and something about the way it rolled loosely over and back made Tobe suspicious.

He sprang forward and leaned over the rock. The brave lay sprawled against a bush, and his eyes stared up at Tobe, black and wicked and unblinking. At the sight Tobe jerked back in terror. But it

was all right. The Indian was good and dead; he knew it.

There the man lay, all smeared up with war paint, with his cruel tomahawk at his waist and a rusty-looking rifle tumbled on the ground beside him. Tobe looked for a long time. He'd made so sure this time they were going to be captured, it was hard to believe they were safe. His heart still jumped around inside his chest like a hop toad in a dry well.

He turned his head and found Mr. Twistletree looking at him. "It's all right," Tobe reassured him. "This here one's dead."

Dead. It seemed strange. An Indian might get killed, shot or scalped. But they didn't just up and die. It was plumb unnatural to find a red man lying out in the bushes, stark and stiff, with not a mark on him.

He reached out a hand, but Mr. Twistletree caught it back. "No, no," he warned. "Don't touch him, Tobias. He may have died of a fever or a plague that left a pestilent miasma."

The naturalist moved around behind the rock and looked the Indian over carefully. "No, it must have been a failure of the heart or lungs, I think. Poor fellow," he added.

"I can't see what's so poor about him," Tobe grunted. "He looks mean enough to me."

"No matter what your color, it is sad to die alone and far from home and those who love you," Mr. Twistletree said. "He was a young man. No doubt he had a wife and little children who will miss him mightily."

Tobe pressed his lips together grimly. "He probably had it in mind to help us die alone and far from home," he reminded the man. "And I don't reckon the thought grieved him." He swung around and pointed with his rifle. "And the rest of his party may be right over there behind them rocks, for all you know."

"They may surely be." Mr. Twistletree nodded. "But so far Providence has been good to us. Let us continue to put our trust in that goodness."

Tobe looked exasperated. Mr. Twistletree was fretful.

"I am aware that we are still in danger, boy," he said. "It ain't always easy for me to remember it, and it may turn out that I will most bitterly regret bringing you here."

He stopped and looked at Tobe soberly. "Most bitterly," he repeated. "But I have to do my best to fulfill my obligations, come what may. However, I will make a bargain with you, Tobias. We will travel three more days, and by noon of the last day I will turn back if we're still unsuccessful."

He took off his spectacles and handed them to Tobe. "There," he said, squinting. "You carry my eyes for me. Now I cannot see birds or flowers or beasts to be drawn from the trail. We will travel steadily there and steadily back."

Tobe grinned. "Naw," he answered. "We'll need my eyes and yours too. We'll stay off the trail when we can, especially at nights. But you got to do what I tell you, Mr. Twistletree. There ain't no point in tempting Providence any further than need be."

His master put his spectacles back on and nodded slowly. "Yes, Tobias, yes, you're right. And I promise to do as you tell me."

Tobe went after the grazing horse, and they set out again. He started to take the Indian's musket. But it wasn't much good. The end of the barrel looked pitted and rusty, and it would take a heap of cleaning. Mr. Twistletree wouldn't likely be able to hit a thing with it anyhow.

"It seems hard to go off and leave him to the foxes and tigers," spoke up Mr. Twistletree, looking back at the Indian.

Tobe grabbed his arm and hustled him off. "We ain't got the time," he said tartly.

At first Tobe had figured he'd have to be after Mr. Twistletree every single minute to hurry up, or have to holler at him not to stray off. He'd reckoned it would be like he was the master and the naturalist was the bound boy. But it didn't turn out so. Mr. Twistletree bent his head and stumbled along the path like a horse pulling a heavy load. He hardly ever looked up. Even when they left the trail and walked in amongst the trees, he kept up a good pace.

Sometimes Tobe would see him reach out and grab a few leaves off a bush when he thought he was unnoticed. And once at night he made a torch of lightwood and went flailing through the bushes after a great greeny long-tailed moth. But Tobe was proud that mostly the naturalist just stepped along across the mountain top and down the far side the way he'd promised he would.

The third day Tobe walked along whistling between his teeth and keeping a mighty close watch on the sun. It was going to be a happy moment when he got to sing out for them to turn around and head back home. And he certainly didn't aim to walk one step further than he had to.

When finally the sun stood high in the sky, Tobe stopped. "Let's turn back," he cried cheerfully.

"No, no," Mr. Twistletree answered. "It's not yet noon. And I spy a river through the trees yonder. If it flows south, it may be the one on my map, and we might be close to the very spot I'm searching for."

There wasn't anything for it but to go on. They plodded along, and finally Tobe asked, "Whatever is this here thing you'd as soon be dead as go home without seeing?"

"Why, I thought I told you it was an ancient fortification," Mr. Twistletree replied. "A bulwark of dirt, a rampart of stone, some kind of old man-made structure."

Tobe pondered a minute. "You mean white men used to live in these parts?" he demanded.

"What makes you think white men built it?" Mr. Twistletree wanted to know.

"Well," Tobe answered slowly. "I never heared tell of Injuns building anything. They don't hardly trouble to make houses for themselves, much less forts. And it don't somehow seem like they need forts, the way they fight."

"Now that's the way my friend in Philadelphia reasons," cried the man in some excitement. "Pish, tush! I tell him that. Pish, tush! What makes him think that these Indians didn't once possess a different and perhaps higher culture than we now behold? Perhaps at one time these were mighty nations of Indians, rich with learning and skills, whose powerful armies went against one another and waged wars until finally, like the ancient Greeks, worn out with battles, they sank from greatness. Or perhaps another people entirely, like those who thrived in Mexico when the Spaniards arrived there, wandered here with their heathen deities and built this fort. And later were wiped out by disease or some act of God."

Tobe grinned at the way Mr. Twistletree was taking on over these things that had all happened so long ago—or might not have happened at all. "Well, how come your friend don't agree with you?" he asked.

Mr. Twistletree twisted up his face. "He thinks Welshmen built it . . . men from across the seas. He believes they discovered America away back before Columbus came along. There is a tale about a Prince Madoc who sailed west from Wales. Nobody knows what became of him, but my friend believes he came here and settled with his followers. He thinks they made this and other fortifications to defend themselves against the Indians, but were defeated and driven away."

Tobe considered this for a while. "Well, what do the Injuns say?" he asked finally. "Who do they say built it?"

"Ah, the old Cherokee who gave my friend this map said the fort was built by a race of moon-eyed people against whom his own ancestors waged a long war."

"Moon-eyed people!" repeated Tobe scornfully. "Whoever heared tell of such! And whatever would moon-eyed folks be anyway?"

"My friend thinks they were the Welshmen. He believes moon-eyed just means blue-eyed, that blue eyes looked to the Indians, who had never seen them before, like a daylight moon, round and pale."

Here Mr. Twistletree grinned slyly and gave a

little wiggle of triumph. "Ah, that's a clever way of phrasing it, clever indeed. But whoever heard of a blue-eyed Welshman? Welshmen are all black, dark-eyed as the Indians themselves."

He studied his map again for a minute. "Of course, it may have been Norsemen. The Vikings perhaps came to this continent long before Prince Madoc, and they would have been more likely to have blue eyes."

"Well, what do you think?" Tobe inquired. "Who do you reckon built this here fort, if'n there's such a thing out here in the woods?"

His master shook his head. "I would have to see it and study it carefully before I could answer that," he replied. "And even then I could do no more than guess."

They pushed on across the river. Mr. Twistletree worried over his map and beat around among the bushes this way and that. At last he sighed heavily and turned to Tobe.

"Boy," he said sadly, "we'll turn back. It's noon and past. I've done my best for my friend and now I'll keep my word with you."

"Well," Tobe said. He looked around, hesitating. "I would dearly love to see this here fort. I reckon there's no need to turn back right this very minute. We could look a mite longer."

Mr. Twistletree didn't say anything. He didn't even smile. But his eyes lit up around the edges, like firelight seeping through the cracks of a closed door. Tobe grinned to himself. The man might have known Tobe wasn't going to give up so easy. A body didn't get a chance to see a fort built by folks with eyes like moons every day in the week.

In the middle of the afternoon they found it, lying between two rivers the way the map showed it. Tobe saw it first, a dirt wall taller than his head by more than a rifle length. It stretched off among the beeches and oaks in both directions. He scrambled to the top and looked back over his shoulder.

"Mr. Twistletree!" he roared and didn't stop to think about Indians at all.

The man came running and panting. Tobe gave him a hand up the wall, and they stood there looking down into the top of a wild plum tree, knobby with little green plums.

"This is it," Mr. Twistletree breathed, and his nose twitched like a dog's.

"I'll be danged," cried Tobe. "I never made it out to be so all-fired big. Somebody went to a heap of trouble to pile up all this dirt."

Mr. Twistletree got down on his knees and poked at the surface of the wall. "And it may be they had a log palisade along the top here," he told Tobe.

He pulled out his ledger book and then thrust it back into his pocket. "Come, Tobias, make haste. Let us see if we can walk around the whole of it before dark."

He trotted off along the wall and then stopped.

"The horse. What shall we do with our skinny old mare? Shall we tie her outside or give her a push over the top?"

Tobe laughed. "There's bound to be a gate. Folks had to get in some way. I'll lead her 'round till we come to a door, and then bring her in."

The entryway wasn't far off. Tobe marveled at it. A long walled alleyway extended back into the fort, and at the end it turned sharply to the left and stopped. There must have been a gate right here at the end at one time, Tobe figured. He could see how tricky this entrance was.

A brave would come running up with his foes close behind him. They would all come streaking into the alleyway, and the warrior would turn to the left and be let in the gate, while his companions rained death and destruction down on his pursuers from the high walls overhead.

Oh, that was the way Injuns did, jumping out at a body when he wasn't expecting it! But surely this fort was too grand for the redskins, for whoever built it, it had taken a power of work and a sight of planning. There was a north wall running from river to river and a south wall just about like it. On the sides the wall ran wherever the land sloped to the water. But where high bluffs made a natural barrier, there wasn't any wall.

Tobe lay looking down at the steep rocks. Not even Injuns could climb up right here. He dropped a pebble down on a little sandy pit, and two killdees flew up, screaming, "Killdee, killdee, killdee!" till it echoed against the cliffs.

Over across the river a big white wading bird with long black legs stood still as a stone in the shallow water. "Looky yonder," he cried to Mr. Twistletree as the bird spread great wings and sailed silently into the twilight. "Looky that crane."

"Heron, boy, heron," corrected Mr. Twistletree absently. He was making a sketch of the fort in his notebook. "Now, look, I've made a blot. Tush!"

It was dark by the time they got back to the entry. "Whoeee, this here's big enough for a good sized farm, thirty, thirty-five acres," Tobe exclaimed as he sat eating a cold turkey wing.

"Oh, aye," the naturalist agreed. "And tomorrow we'll see what we can find of the people who built it. The Cherokees say these moon-eyed folks lived underground. Maybe we can find one of their burrows."

The moon rose, and Tobe, lying on the blanket beside Mr. Twistletree, stared at it as it floated free of the beeches. What kind of people could it be who had eyes like moons and lived in holes in the ground? Maybe tomorrow they'd know, maybe tomorrow they'd make some strange and wonderful discovery.

They spent a good many warm June days in the fort. It gave Tobe a queer feeling, half-scared, half-excited, to be forted up there in Indian country and the red men not even suspecting. Why, a body could live here the year round and the Indians not know! He wouldn't have to shoot game at all unless he was a mind to. A body could do like Tobe, kill squirrels and groundhogs and a turkey or two by throwing rocks.

Tobe snared rabbits and caught fish with his bare hands in the clear rocky streams. There were late strawberries in a big patch along one riverbank, and sarvisberries were beginning to ripen. Mr. Twistletree knew a heap of roots and leaves that were good to eat. Tobe didn't take much to the greens, but some of the roots, baked in ashes, were fine, as good as potatoes or corn.

Tobe and his master dug here and there in the fort and sometimes into the side of the walls. But they found no underground houses and no signs of who had built the structure. A few arrowheads, a bone or two, a handful of mussel shells—anybody might have left those here any time.

"It don't matter too much," Mr. Twistletree told Tobe one evening as they lay watching the fireflies flickering along the riverbank and listening to the chuck-will's-widow. "If we were to find a carved stone tablet saying, 'This fort was built in 1533 by English soldiers,' my friend in Philadelphia would go right on believing what he wanted to."

"Like old Pliny, huh?" asked Tobe. "But I reckon

this place is older than that, Mr. Twistletree. Them beeches growing on the wall is mighty big. And it takes a heap of time for a beech to get that big."

The man nodded. "Oh, this is an ancient place, Tobias. Ancient and mysterious. I've felt it more than once sitting with the great quiet walls all around, trying to imagine what went on here."

Tobe felt his spine prickle. If a body believed in ghosts, he might figure there was a whole crowd of them here. He might figure right this minute they were watching Asa Twistletree and Tobias Bledsoe. And maybe they didn't exactly like having two live people poking around in here, Tobe thought uneasily.

"Well," Mr. Twistletree said, moving toward their bed, followed closely by the boy, "I've done my best for my friend and tomorrow we'll leave."

Tobe woke early the next morning. It was going to be a fine day, a good day for traveling. All around him rose up the round sweet voices of thrushes. It was a funny thing. Tobe reckoned he'd heard those birds sing all his life, but he'd never really listened to them till Mr. Twistletree made him. It just didn't seem possible a bird could sound so tarnal pretty.

He could recollect once seeing his mam sitting by a spring listening to a bird singing. He couldn't recall the song, but it might have been a thrush. He remembered the time because it was the day they'd left Salisbury to go to Kentuck. His mam hadn't complained a mite, but seeing her sitting there listening, he'd known how much she hated to leave the snug little cabin at Salisbury and go off into wild country.

Tobe, however, was anxious to be on the move now. He didn't relish the thought of traveling back through Indian country. But since it had to be done, a body might as well get it over with while the weather was good.

And Mr. Twistletree was ready enough to go. It was just that it was hard for him to leave any place. He stuffed the ledger in his saddlebag with the bird skins and tested the thongs around the bundle of roots and leaves. And that was all the packing up he had to do. But he wasn't set to leave yet. There was a snake sunning itself on the rocks by the river, and he needs must go see what kind it was.

When they were within ten feet of it, the snake roused itself and slipped off the rocks. Tobe heard the dry buzzing rattle and drew back. "That there's a rattlesnake and a big one," he said. "Come on away."

But Mr. Twistletree ran forward. "Bring a stick," he cried. "Bring a stick, Tobias! Hurry, hurry!"

Tobe was surprised. He'd never known Mr. Twistletree to kill a snake. He grabbed up a stick and ran toward him.

"Stand back," the boy called. "I'll whop him a good one."

Mr. Twistletree hopped up and down. "No, no,

don't kill him," he squealed. "Pin his head down, so he can't bite."

Tobe did as he was told. He reckoned Mr. Twistletree had some scheme in mind, but he was astounded when the man reached down and seized the big snake by its head and its tail.

It writhed and whipped around till Tobe made sure it would get away. But Mr. Twistletree held it fast. He stumbled over the rocks to a deep pool, then raised the snake over his head, and flung it down into the water.

"I've always wanted to see if a big rattler like this could swim," he panted. "Look, Tobias, it floats like a bladder and swims as well as any water snake."

Tobe stepped forward among the rocks. There was a warning buzz; something fell heavily against his leg. An icy sweat of fear and pain rolled over him. He glanced down fearfully at the thing clinging to his deerskin breeches.

"Mr. Twistletree!" he screamed. "I been bit!"

Ten

Tobe beat wildly at the snake where it twisted and writhed against his leg, but still it clung. It was maddening to see that mouth stretched so wide, to feel those needle-sharp fangs in his leg. He kicked out, hoping to sling the rattler off. But it was useless, he could see now, for the varmint's teeth were caught in his leather breeches.

He screamed again and grabbed the thick scaly body and jerked and jerked. The fangs went scraping up and down his leg.

"Wait!" yelled Mr. Twistletree, clambering across the rocks toward him.

Tobe hardly heard. The snake had coiled halfway up his arm and the rattlers shimmered before his eyes. He tugged fiercely, his breath jolting out of him in great sobs. He twisted, he turned, he squeezed that fat body till it suddenly was loose, wriggling in his hands.

He threw it down heavily against a stone and then stamped on its arrow-shaped head. A shock of pain

passed all through him every time his foot came down, but he didn't stop.

"Boy!" cried Mr. Twistletree, gripping his shoulder. "Boy!"

Tobe stood still, shuddering and gasping. There was a fiery ache in his leg that throbbed and stabbed till he was dizzy. He put out a hand to steady himself.

The naturalist half-carried, half-dragged the boy up the bank and stretched him out in the shade. With a knife he ripped off the breeches leg and slashed across the leg where it had begun to swell. Then he began to squeeze the bite gently.

Tobe bolted up, shrieking, "Don't! Don't touch me. I can't stand it no more."

But Mr. Twistletree pressed again and wiped away the yellowish fluid. Groaning, Tobe pulled away and thrashed about on the moss. The man jumped up, ripped open the bundle, and began to search through the leaves and roots frantically.

"Here, Tobias, chew these leaves," he ordered, returning.

Tobe stared at him with dazed eyes, and the naturalist stuffed the leaves into the boy's mouth. "It's black snakeroot," Mr. Twistletree told him. "It's a certain cure, I've been told. Chew now, boy."

Tobe tried, but his jaws didn't seem to work. Mr. Twistletree chewed some himself and then spread the wet lump over the bite and scratches.

"There, boy," he said soothingly. "Snakeroot inside and out. You'll mend in no time."

Tobe could hardly hear him. Everything was changing. Mr. Twistletree had disappeared and Tobe himself was no longer there. All that was left of him was a great ugly shape of hurt. Oh, he was dying; he knew he was!

The trees overhead were full of faces that looked down at him. "He's a-dying," said one of the faces.

"No. No, I ain't either," Tobe cried, and he tried to struggle up, but he was too weak to move.

His sister Tildy peered down at him, her red hair spread out behind her in a leafy cloud. The hair waved up and down, twisted and smoked, burst into flames.

"You're afire," Tobe gasped. "Look out, Tildy, you're afire."

"Hit don't matter none," Tildy answered. "I'm a fire dragon and I like it." And she ran out a long forked tongue and hissed at him gently.

Mr. Twistletree put a poultice of something on his leg, something cool, and the cold spread all through him, an aching, numbing chill that made him shiver from top to toe.

"Mammy," he cried. "Charlie's snatched all the kivers and it's a-snowing. I'm cold, Mam; I'm a-dying of cold."

His mam bent over him and she was wearing spectacles like Mr. Twistletree. "Hush, boy," she said in Mr. Twistletree's rasping voice. "Hush, now, and rest."

"Don't leave me," Tobe begged. "Don't leave me here to die far from home. I'm afeared."

But she was gone. A dim mistiness was everywhere, and his leg hurt terribly. He remembered now, he was drowning, drowning in the Clinch River and that was a cramp in his leg. Or was it a snake in his leg? He couldn't remember and it was too late, too late, too late. Darkness swallowed him up.

When he opened his eyes, Mr. Twistletree was sitting beside him, writing in his ledger book. "Is it time to go?" Tobe asked, startled. He struggled to sit up, but he was weak as bread and water, and one of his legs hurt as if it were broken.

"Don't move," Mr. Twistletree commanded. He fetched some broth in a wooden bowl.

Tobe stared at the cedar vessel in surprise. "I must of been sick a good spell to give old Twistletree time to whittle out that," he thought. It was a pure wonder Mr. Twistletree had been able to carve it at all, awkward as the man was. It wasn't much bowl, all rough and lopsided, but Tobe could drink out of it and that was all that mattered.

The broth was good, rabbit cooked down and thickened with some of the roots the naturalist knew about. Tobe was powerful hungry.

"Not too much," the naturalist cautioned. "It ain't

good to eat too much when you've had nothing for more than two days."

"Two days!" cried out Tobe. "You aim to say I been lying right here two whole days?"

"Aye, out of your head most of the time too." The man nodded. "And you'll lie here a good while longer before you can travel, bad off as that leg still is."

He was right. Tobe's leg felt big as a flatboat, and he couldn't even wiggle his toes. He reckoned he'd just have to lie there and make the best of it.

At first he did a heap of sleeping, but by and by he was slept out. Then he had to sit and stare around at the bushes while Mr. Twistletree went off to set traps for rabbits or try to shoot a turkey. Time dragged then, snail-slow, hour after hour.

It wasn't that the man meant to leave him alone so long, Tobe knew—only that he'd get to watching some beetle or drawing some flower and forget that time was slipping by.

"There's one good thing about learning your letters," Tobe told himself. "If'n you have to set and do nothing, you can practice saying your letters."

He could say all his letters and spell his name and cipher a little too now. Two and five is seven, seven and three is ten, anybody could do that. What he liked was the timeses. Two times six is twelve, two times twelve is twenty-four. Figures seemed exciting and wonderful going on and on that way, with no end to them, and yet always neatly doing just what they were meant to do.

More than half of June had gone and his leg was still swollen and mottled blue and yellow. It made him sweat and shake to hobble the short distance to the spring.

"Let the sun shine on it," Mr. Twistletree told him. "The sun is the prime healer."

So, Tobe sat alone on the riverbank with his leg stuck out into the hot, bright sunlight. The water murmured to itself, a little brown bird went teeter-tottering around among the rocks, and Tobe said his AB-ab's.

"T-O-B-I-A-S, Tobias," he spelt out. "T like this, and O is round, and B—whichaway does B go?"

He couldn't remember whether the humps stuck out to the right or the left. With his hand he wrote the letter in the air, trying it out to see what looked proper for a B. He made a straight line and then he shaped the first hump. And that was as far as he got. His hand stayed up in the air.

For there, looking through that loop of the B, was a narrow hard face, copper-skinned and black-eyed. Silently it stared at Tobe until at last he dropped his hand. Slowly, slowly, he reached out for his rifle where it lay on the sunny rocks. His numb fingers had just touched it, had just closed over the lock, when a big moccasined foot crunched down on his wrist.

Eleven

At first Tobe couldn't believe it. "It's another one of them fever dreams," he told himself. "It ain't real; I know it ain't."

Even when two Indians tied his hands and feet, he'd scarcely been able to credit it. It was like he wasn't the one captured, but some other body watching the whole thing happen from a great distance away.

There were three of the red men. He watched dully while they poked among the few belongings Mr. Twistletree had left scattered about. One of them had Tobe's rifle and was looking it over, mighty pleased. The others ripped open the saddle-bags and the bundle and scattered the leaves and roots and bird skins everywhere, trampling them underfoot, angry at finding such useless truck.

Now one of them had got Mr. Twistletree's ledger book. He held it up curiously and peered at the notes and drawings, rubbing his fingers over the sheets.

The one with Tobe's rifle had snatched up the

skin of a big red-crested woodcock and slipped it on his hand. He worked the bright head back and forth and gave the bird's loud mocking cry. Then he ran up to the brave with the ledger book and began to peck at the pages.

The other brave slapped him away with the ledger, and one of the pages fluttered away among the bushes. One by one he pulled out the other leaves and threw them into the breeze.

Tobe groaned to see them drifting away on the river and flapping against the rocks. A power of work had gone into the ledger book. He knew how careful Mr. Twistletree had been to get everything just right and so. And now, in the blink of an eye, it was all gone, ruined.

The only thing the Indians didn't touch was the rattler Tobe had killed. Mr. Twistletree had brought it up from the river right after Tobe had got back in his right mind. "Here, Tobias," he had said. "Here's your old enemy brought low indeed. Maybe the sight of him will give you strength."

Now it lay, a coil of skin and skeleton on the rocks. The Indians looked at it, but they didn't touch it. Tobe had heard tell Indians thought a heap of rattlesnakes and he reckoned it must be so, seeing the way they kept away from it, as if to walk beside the carcass would offend the snake somehow.

"Well, they can thank this one here for two prisoners," he muttered. "We'd have been long gone from here but for him waiting in the rocks for me to step on him."

No, that wasn't true. They wouldn't have been here at all if Tobe hadn't told Mr. Twistletree to keep on hunting for the fort. Why hadn't he kept quiet? It had been none of his worry.

Maybe he had no right to lay the fault on anyone, on Mr. Twistletree who'd made a foolish bargain, on his own father who figured to get rich by binding out his oldest boy, on himself for not looking where he set his foot. Maybe they were all to blame, but what difference did it make? He had been caught by the Chickamaugas, good and proper, and he was going to be burned alive!

It came over him then in a heavy black blanket of fear and despair that almost suffocated him. He clenched his jaws to keep from howling and flinging himself around in panic. He wouldn't let the savages know how scared he was, not if he shook wide open with fright. He stared off across the river, trying hard to make the blood stop pounding in his ears.

He hoped Mr. Twistletree would get away. Likely the naturalist would die in the woods, lost, without food or a gun and not much sense. But it was better than giving the Indians the satisfaction of killing him. The Chickamaugas would do it the cruelest way—rip out your fingernails, heap hot coals on your bare feet—

He clenched his fists. "No, no, no!" he cried silently. "I won't think about it."

Just then he saw Mr. Twistletree. His master came dilly-dallying through the woods, looking at this, that, and the other. Tobe would have yelled out a warning, but he couldn't. His tongue clove to the roof of his mouth, and all he was able to do was gag and swallow.

It wouldn't do any good to warn the naturalist anyway. If he yelled "Injuns!" Mr. Twistletree would likely come running up to draw a picture of them.

The man stumbled along among the bushes, and suddenly he gave a yell. "My ledger book!" he shrieked. "My ledger book!"

He ran here and there gathering up the precious pages right at the Indians' feet without even noticing them. The tall one with Tobe's rifle stopped him finally, grabbing him by the shoulder.

Mr. Twistletree looked up dazedly. "My notes, my ledger book," he moaned.

He jerked away, running off after another of the pages. The Indian ran after him and stuck the rifle between his legs so that Mr. Twistletree tripped and fell. The warrior kicked him once and snatched him to his feet. Slipping the ramrod from under the rifle barrel, he commenced to beat the man across the shoulders.

Mr. Twistletree stood still with the pages clutched

to his chest, and the blows rained down over him. His spectacles fell off, and the Indian left off hitting him and picked up the eyeglasses. He looked at them carefully, felt the glass between his thumb and finger, squinted through them, and then stuck them on his nose. The others ran up to see.

Mr. Twistletree stayed with head bowed, right where he'd been left and never made a murmur.

Even when he was lying beside Tobe later, tied up tight and with the red men all about him, he didn't seem to see or hear them or notice where he was. He was still mourning his book, Tobe knew. It was gone for sure now, most of it used to get the wood burning.

The braves moved around their campfire, talk-

ing together and cooking some deer meat and hardly even noticing their prisoners. The tall one passed the spectacles around, and they all tried them on for the hundredth time, staring at different things and shaking their heads and rubbing their eyes at what they saw.

At last they stretched out and went to sleep. As it grew darker, Mr. Twistletree roused himself. He turned his head and stared at Tobe.

"Tobias," he said heavily. "Are you harmed in any manner? I am truly sorry that I let myself be so carried away by concern for my material possessions. My first thought should have been for you."

"It wouldn't of done much good," Tobe answered bitterly. "You and me can do all the thinking about each other we've a mind to, and it won't change matters a jot. If'n you could think up a company of militia with rifles aplenty, that might be some help. But nothing else ain't going to save our skins."

Mr. Twistletree said nothing more. Tobe figured there was nothing more to say. The fire gutted out slowly, and overhead Tobe could make out seven bright stars.

"Up yonder's Charles's Wain, like Mr. Twistletree showed me. And if'n I hadn't been snake bit, I could get loose from here right this minute and find my way north by it," he thought.

For a minute he felt almost hopeful. But he couldn't break these leather thongs that held him. And even if he did, he knew his leg was still too weak and painful to travel on. There was no need to think about it.

Sometimes, when he'd been traveling with his pappy and they'd been out on the trail at night, he'd made out what he'd do if Indians came after them —how he'd fight to save his life, and how if he got captured, he'd be so quick and smart to escape.

Oh, it was easy enough to figure out, lying there with his folks all around him and two good legs to run on and his rifle close at hand.

But didn't things always work out different than he thought they would? Hadn't he planned how he'd come marching home with Mr. Twistletree, ready to show his mam what a good scribe he was, ready to tickle Charlie and Tildy and the others with tales about what had happened to him, about the fire dragon and stones that burned and all the rest?

And now—he stared up at the sky. He might have cried, but his eyes were hot and dry. Anger and fear and misery had dried up his juices, the way the sun had dried the rattlesnake.

Charles's Wain circled overhead and at last Tobe slept.

Twelve

Tobe opened his eyes. He could see daylight through the cracks in the roof of the cabin. For just a moment he thought he was back on the Holston River. But this was no white man's cabin he was in; this was an Indian cabin deep in Chickamauga territory.

He sat up carefully, for he was stiff and sore from riding the old mare. A day and a half they'd spent traveling, with Tobe clinging to the mare's back, giddy with the pain in his leg. Mr. Twistletree had had to hold him on most of the way.

The old nag herself had reached here half dead from toting him and two deer carcasses. And the flies, flocking around and biting, had worried even the Indians. Tobe had never reckoned to be so almighty glad to see a spot where he was going to be burned to death, but he had been.

He looked around for Mr. Twistletree. The man was sleeping on the hard clay floor, and Tobe wished he still was. A body could hardly wake up to a darker day than the one that lay ahead of them.

He dragged himself over to the wall and put his eye to one of the cracks. Who would have thought Dragging Canoe's town that he'd heard such a heap about would turn out to be such a sorry-looking place? There were some mud and cane huts and one or two other log cabins like this one, whomper-jawed and sag-roofed. It was a dreary place, but Tobe figured he could die as well here as in a fine town.

A heap of dogs and young 'uns tangled in the dust. Girls walked by carrying water or loads of kindling wood. Women with stone hoes trudged out toward the fields that Tobe could just make out beyond the last huts. A woman with a white man's shirt over her dress ground away at something on a flat stone— corn, Tobe reckoned. He'd seen his mother and sisters make meal that way when they had no decent mortar to pound it in.

"I wisht I knew if Ma was all right," he thought suddenly. "By this time I reckon Pa's figured out something to do with the money Mr. Twistletree give him for me. Likely it's all gone and I know in reason they never got a garden in. Charlie ain't hardly good for toting wood and water, much less digging or hoeing."

He'd had a good spot in mind for beans and corn and turnips. He'd have had to work hard to get the ground ready and the seed in, but he'd have managed.

Maybe Tildy had done some of it. Maybe Tildy

and his mother had raised enough for them to get by on. Betsy wouldn't help, he knew. All Pa's dreams that came to naught had made Betsy sullen and hateful. She never did anything if she could keep from it.

Behind him he heard Mr. Twistletree stirring. "Be you all right, Tobias?" his master asked.

Tobe grimaced. He was all right. His leg ached, but he wasn't swimmy-headed any longer. "I'm fine," he answered shortly.

Mr. Twistletree got up and came over to him. He put his face down close to the boy's leg and squinted at the bad place. "It ain't as bad as I expected," he said at last. "There's some swelling but not much inflammation."

"I don't reckon it makes a heap of difference," Tobe said. "I just wisht I had some water, that's all."

Mr. Twistletree sighed and sat down and closed his eyes. Tobe felt sorry for him. "I reckon he's scared too, the way I am," he thought. "Maybe it's worse not to be able to see than to have a lame leg."

He stood up and limped around restlessly. He'd seen a wolf in a cage once, pacing up and down, up and down. That was the way he felt now. He'd almost rather the Indians came after them right this minute than to have to wait this way, not knowing anything and worrying.

He stared out between the cracks once more. There were a heap of horses lined up over yonder, like somebody was getting ready to go somewhere.

He hadn't noticed them before and wondered what it meant.

Maybe they were going to take him and Mr. Twistletree somewhere else. Maybe they were going to fetch some friends from the other villages to see the fun.

He sat down suddenly. He wished he didn't know all the things the Chickamaugas did to their prisoners—sticking flaming pine splinters under their skin and making them dance on hot coals. His stomach knotted and his palms ran with sweat.

If they just had a chance to get away! A man and a boy in a half-doty log cabin ought to be able to escape easy enough. But they'd never get out of the village if one was lame and the other nearly blind, he reckoned. Not if one was Tobias Bledsoe and the other was Asa Twistletree.

He crouched with his head on his knees and tried not to think about anything—anything at all. It was hard not to think about anything. "A, B, C, D, E," he said over to himself, trying hard to picture the letters and to keep other things out of his head. "H, J, K . . ."

No, something came before J. What was the letter? Was that somebody coming? "J, K, L—" He would have to begin again.

There was a racket right outside, and he started up. They were coming now, for a fact, coming to get the prisoners.

"Mr. Twistletree!" he gasped. "Don't you know

no plants we could kill ourselves with or something? I don't want to burn. Don't let 'em burn me!"

"Hush, hush, Tobias," commanded Mr. Twistletree. His face stood out in the dimness as white as a new blaze on the side of a tree.

Somebody was fumbling at the door. Tobe's heart bumped in his chest, faster than the pounding of a sweep mill.

"Who is it? Who is it?" squeaked Mr. Twistletree, half rising as the door swung open.

"It ain't but a squaw," breathed Tobe. "It ain't but a squaw with some food and water." He was a little ashamed. He had no right to act like he had just then. Whatever lay in store for them, there was no help for it, and they'd both have to bear it the best way they could.

Tobe was powerful thirsty and hungry too. The food, stew in a clay pot, was greasy and full of burnt meat and hard beans. Tobe ate his share hurriedly, gulping down the lumps, not caring to know what they were.

The water was cool and clear. There was some trash in it, but Tobe fished the twigs out of the big gourd and drank deeply. It tasted so sweet, a body might close his eyes and believe he was somewhere else, not lame, not a prisoner, but free, drinking out of any spring he was a mind to.

The woman watched sullenly while they ate. Then she gathered up the vessels and went out. She didn't close the door behind her, and the sight was enough to make Tobe split open with rage. "They know we ain't got a chance to get away," he told himself grimly. "They don't have to tie us up or shut the door or nothing."

Well, they'd best not count on it too much. He just might wake up tomorrow and find his leg strong again and he'd slide out that open door as quick as an otter down a mud bank. Only it wouldn't happen. He might as well give up hoping anything good would happen to him. He moved over to the doorway, sat down and looked out. What he saw made him jump like a rabbit.

That was *him,* Dragging Canoe himself. Oh, Tobe would know him anywhere! He'd heard folks speak of him, tall and hook-nosed as a hawk, pock-marked, with a limp from a wound he'd got fighting the whites years ago.

"There goes the Canoe," Tobe whispered.

Mr. Twistletree came up behind him and squinted out. He shook his head. "What does he look like?" he asked.

"Ugly," the boy replied. But to himself he couldn't help but admit Dragging Canoe looked the way a chief ought to look, strong and proud and fierce.

And suddenly the Canoe's eyes swept over the hut and rested on the prisoners. Tobe could almost feel that glance touch him, and he shrank back. Oh, there was a wicked heart and no mistake! The chief walked on to the horses.

"Yonder's one of them braves that captured us and he's wearing your glasses dangling from his silly ear," Tobe told Mr. Twistletree. "He's almighty proud of them, the way he's swaggering about. And I reckon you'll never get 'em back."

Mr. Twistletree blinked. "You'll have to be my eyes now, Tobias," he said.

They were all mounted except the Canoe, and Tobe was glad when the chief got on his horse and rode off.

"There they all go," he said.

"Where could they be going?" Mr. Twistletree asked.

"I don't know and don't care," answered Tobe. "The more ground there is between me and the Canoe, the better I like it."

But who was that coming yonder, that little fat important-looking fellow in the green blanket? What did he want to come waddling over this way for? Tobe watched uneasily.

The little Indian came straight for the cabin. He was an old man, with streaks of gray in his black hair and a pair of scissors on a string around his neck like some bauble a lady might wear. He stepped inside the door and took Mr. Twistletree by the arm. "Come," he said fiercely.

Mr. Twistletree held back, squinting at the Indian. "What? What?" he rasped.

"Wait," Tobe cried, struggling to get to his feet. The little man held up a hand. "Boy stay," he commanded. He pulled the naturalist roughly out the door. "Man come."

Tobe watched till they disappeared among the huts. Whatever did the Indian want? And how come he took just Mr. Twistletree?

Tobe backed away from the door and sat down. The minutes went dragging by, and he shifted about, dejected and uneasy. Who would have thought he'd miss his master like this? But he did. Skinny and half blind Mr. Twistletree might be; at least he was company. And somehow having him around seemed to perk up Tobe's spirits.

Somebody giggled. He looked up to see the door of the cabin crowded with brown faces—mostly little young 'uns, naked as jay birds, but some boys his own age or even older in deerskin flaps.

One of them spat at him, and Tobe glared back. A rock came sailing into the cabin and he ducked. One of the older boys stepped inside. He was grinning and he had a knife. Tobe didn't like the looks of it, though it wasn't but a flint-rock knife.

He reached behind him and picked up the rock. The boy with the knife said some Indian word and twisted his knife in the air. The others pushed up behind him, edging him closer to Tobe.

"Don't you come no closer," muttered Tobe. "I'll bust out your teeth with this here rock."

The Indian boy sneered. He brandished the knife in front of him and took a sudden step toward Tobe, grinning widely. Tobe raised the rock and threw it hard. It landed on the boy's chest with a thud, and the grin was gone. He shouted something and rushed at Tobe.

Tobe kicked with his good leg. But the boy was quick. He jumped out of the way and fell on Tobe with a wild scream. Tobe grabbed at the knife, but the Indian's weight pushed him flat on his back and he couldn't reach it.

Now the rest of the Indians rushed in and grabbed his feet. Tobe kicked and thrashed about and struck out with his fists. They swarmed all over him, sat on his legs, and tried to hold his arms. They hit and scratched and poked. Still Tobe fought back, twisting an arm or leg loose occasionally to get in a blow.

The boy with the knife sat on his chest and, holding Tobe's hair with one hand, sawed away at his scalp. The knife was dull, but it hurt a heap. Tobe hollered and jerked his head away. Somebody put a hand over his mouth, and he chomped down on it for all he was worth, grinding his teeth into the meat.

There was a howl, and Tobe bit all the harder. The howl grew louder, and somebody grabbed his throat, choking him to make him open his mouth. He couldn't get his breath. He opened his jaws, sucking in air. The Indian who had been bitten jumped up and ran out.

Somebody outside shouted, and the rest of the little Indians scurried away. The boy with the knife slashed one last time at Tobe's head. He spat in Tobe's face and was gone.

"Bring your mammy next time. Maybe she's got a knife that can cut," Tobe bawled after him.

He turned on his side and wept with rage and helplessness. He wished they'd gone on and killed him. He was too wretched to keep living. By now Mr. Twistletree was dead and they'd have scalped him the way a white man might skin a squirrel, thinking no more of it. He pounded the wall with his fist. Wasn't there any way he could get away, any way at all?

Through his tears he watched a little blue-tailed skink slipping in and out of the logs, pushing among the curling ends of bark. "Go on out," he whispered fiercely. "It's easy enough for you. Git on out. I don't want to see you no more."

He lay watching the shadows grow longer and longer. It might be he would never again see the day come to an end, see the shadows deepen under the oak trees or the tops of the sycamores bow and turn in the breeze that sprang up.

He turned stiffly at a noise behind him. Mr. Twistletree was standing in the door.

"Mr. Twistletree!" he exclaimed. "I made sure you was dead."

"No, no," Mr. Twistletree said softly, coming into the room. "I'm fine, Tobias, fine. He thought I was a white medicine man. And my boy, we're free!

We can leave tomorrow. They'll give us food and a gun and we can leave. Here, lad, I've fetched some food and water and a salve for your leg. Do you suppose you can walk on it tomorrow?"

Tobe picked up the pot of water and drank before he answered. He was too surprised to say anything anyway, for he could hardly believe what his master told him. They couldn't just walk off and leave the Indians. There was a trick to it somehow. It was just another way of being cruel to them.

He wiped his mouth. "I was powerful thirsty," he said at last.

"Didn't you hear me, boy?" the man asked. "We can leave tomorrow!"

"How come they're going to let us go?" inquired Tobe.

"Listen," said Mr. Twistletree. "Fourteen, fifteen years ago a naturalist named William Bartram from Philadelphia came into the Cherokee country. Mr. Bartram is a good man and he knows a very great deal about plants. Why, in his garden, where I have been many times, there are plants from . . ."

"Don't tell me that," begged Tobe. "Tell me about getting away from here."

"Yes, well, Mr. Bartram lived among the southern Indians for some years. He met this man called the Hummingbird, at a Cherokee town somewhere and they became fast friends," Mr. Twistletree went on. "Mr. Bartram wanted the Hummingbird to come to Philadelphia and visit him, and the Indian promised he would. But then Hummingbird had a powerful dream, he said, that bade him come here and live with Dragging Canoe and fight for the return of all lands to the Indians."

He sighed sadly. "He and Mr. Bartram had some fine times though, and Hummingbird has never forgotten him. And because I know William Bartram, the Hummingbird is my friend and will let us go."

Tobe could feel hope rising up in him as warm as the summer's sun. But he wanted to be sure. He would never reach the point where he could trust Chickamaugas.

"Where's Dragging Canoe? This here is his town, ain't it? How come old Hummingbird to take over all of a sudden?" he asked.

"The Canoe has gone to some Creek town far from here on business," Mr. Twistletree told him. "The other chiefs are at a treaty meeting and that makes Hummingbird the man of authority, I gather." He laughed suddenly. "He tells me that he is not afraid of Dragging Canoe because he knows the Canoe will die next spring after a scalp dance. The Hummingbird has some kind of stone crystal in which he can see future happenings."

Mr. Twistletree stopped and frowned. "It's your leg that worries me now, Tobias," he said anxiously. "Do you think you will be able to walk? I'm quite certain they won't furnish a horse for us." He dropped down and began to rub some of the salve he had brought into the boy's leg.

"It ain't too bad," Tobe answered. "I reckon to get away from Dragging Canoe's town I could walk on my hands or elbows, for a fact." It was true. He'd leave, given the chance. He didn't aim to let anything hold them back. He'd get away from Chickamauga country if he had to carry his leg under his arm.

He could hardly sleep that night for thinking about it. "I won't never go off again," he promised himself. "There ain't no call to bind me out another time. I'll get a piece of land all my own and build me a cabin on it. And Ma can stay there if Pa aims to go traipsing off somewheres."

Early the next morning he was up and sitting at the door, waiting for the old medicine man.

They waited a long spell. There weren't many Indians about. Some children passed the cabin and stared sulkily at Tobe. One of them had a long scratch down his face. Tobe looked quickly away. He didn't want any of them starting any trouble with him now.

Still no one came. Tobe was hungry. There'd only been a smidgin of food to share last night, and none at all this morning. They drank what was left of the water. Mr. Twistletree inspected Tobe's leg, and they both agreed it was much better and that he could walk on it.

The morning wore on. Tobe was well nigh out of

his skin with waiting, though he tried not to show it. "Maybe he just means for us to leave," he suggested.

"No, no," Mr. Twistletree answered fretfully. "Hummingbird said he would provide us with food and a gun. And we must have them. We'll have to wait."

Along about noon, Tobe said, "Yonder he comes now."

That was just like an Injun. Tobe reckoned he'd enjoyed keeping the whites waiting, giving them the jittering shakes while he giggled watching them. The old man carried a packet of something and an old musket.

He walked straight up to Mr. Twistletree and thrust these things into his hands. "Take these," he said. "Leave now. Injun show way."

"Well, I . . . I thank you kindly," Mr. Twistletree stammered. "I will go straight to Mr. William Bartram's house and tell him how well we have been treated by you. I will tell him what a wise and great man the Hummingbird is."

The Hummingbird smiled and shut his eyes a minute to show that he agreed entirely.

"Come along, Tobias," Mr. Twistletree commanded. "We'll set out at once. You take the gun."

But the Hummingbird reached out a rough hand and caught Tobe by the arm. "No, not go," he cried harshly. "Man go. Boy stay here, be punished."

Thirteen

Mr. Twistletree went white as a ghost. The gun dropped from his hands at Tobe's feet. "No!" he cried out. "No, this is my bound boy and I must have him with me."

Tobe stared. He couldn't rightly take it in.

The Hummingbird said nothing. His face looked as set and hard as the clay floor.

Mr. Twistletree swallowed and began again. "I . . . I . . . Mr. Bartram wants to see him when we get back," he said. "This boy *has* to come to Philadelphia with me!"

"Boy stay," repeated the Hummingbird.

Tobe could feel the angry blood creep up his chest and neck. Oh, he must have been lightheaded, for a fact, to think the Chickamaugas would let him go so easily!

"Why does this boy have to stay?" Mr. Twistletree persisted. "He is as innocent of intent to harm as I am—as Mr. Bartram was," he added. "In fact, he is more so because he would not have come here at all if I had not brought him. Why, why must he be punished?"

"It don't matter," Tobe muttered between his clenched teeth. "Don't go a-begging him. He ain't fixing to let me go. You go on, Mr. Twistletree . . . you . . ." He stopped. Injun meanness was reason enough for letting one go and making the other stay. His master might as well leave. There was nothing he could say to change things.

There was a long silence. Tobe looked up and was surprised to see the Hummingbird searching around for words, his face screwed up in thought. The old man must think a heap of Mr. Bartram, whoever he was, and of Mr. Twistletree too, to try and tell them why.

"Time ago back," the Hummingbird began slowly, "six braves go on warpath. One was Snake-who-sleeps. This brave had bad dreams . . . had witches in belly . . . turned back. No fight . . . let others go fight. Five braves come back . . . here . . . with many scalps. Where Snake-who-sleeps? Not here. Where? Five braves find him . . . find white trail too."

He paused and pointed to Mr. Twistletree and then to Tobe. "Find man, find boy, find horse foot in ground around brave. Find Snake-who-sleeps dead."

The Hummingbird turned. His eyes, hard and black as little stones, bored into Tobe's. "*He* kill Snake-who-sleeps."

"I never!" Tobe shouted. "No! Ask Mr. Twistle-tree."

"Oh, we did see a warrior who had died on the trail," spoke out Mr. Twistletree. "We didn't harm him. He was dead when we found him. No one killed him; he died of disease."

"Braves read sign," the Hummingbird said knowingly. "Boy kill Injun."

"I never laid a finger on him, and you know it!" cried Tobe.

"Injun braves know. Tell me," the Hummingbird went on. "You got bad leg. You know why? Snake old honored friend with Injun. White boy kill Injun . . . snake love Injun . . . snake follow white boy . . . bite good."

He paused, looking pleased. "Bite good, hurt much," he continued. "Boy no run away. Injun find boy . . . bring him back to village. Boy bad, bad . . . be punished. Snake knows this . . . snake help."

A sort of pain, made out of fury and helplessness, twisted through Tobe. Oh, wasn't that just like Injuns? He'd never harmed a living one of them, much as he might have wanted to. But because a snake had had the bad luck to bite him, he thought scornfully, they took it as a sure sign he'd killed every Chickamauga for miles around. He shouldn't have counted such a heap on getting away. A body ought never to look forward to something good happening to him. He ought to expect the worst because nine times out of ten, that's what was going to happen to him. He'd learned that much in eleven years.

The Hummingbird bent and swiftly picked up the gun.

"But the boy didn't hurt your warrior, I tell you," Mr. Twistletree exclaimed, grabbing the Indian by the arm. "Can't you believe that from me?"

The medicine man stared at Mr. Twistletree for a moment. Then he held out the gun. "You good man I know," he spoke. "Take gun and go. Leave boy. Be happy . . . go Phil'delphy."

Mr. Twistletree drew back. He turned first red and then very pale, and the cords in his neck stood out more than ever.

"No, no! I'll stay," and his voice shook a little. "I'll stay here with my bound boy. I cannot leave him alone. Take your gun back. It was not given in friendship. You cared not for William Bartram or for me. Take it, take it and go!".

The Hummingbird turned on his heels and shuffled out. He looked back once, then slammed and fastened the door.

Mr. Twistletree stepped over to one side of the cabin and sat down.

"It . . . I . . ." Tobe began and stopped. What could he say? "It . . . it was just an old musket; likely we couldn't of killed a sitting groundhog with it."

He stared wretchedly up into a corner of the cabin. "You should of gone on, Mr. Twistletree,"

he blurted out at last. "You should of got away whilst you had the chance and sent somebody after me from the Holston settlement, White's Fort, or Campbell's Station or somewheres."

Mr. Twistletree shook his head. "Nay," he answered. "They'd have . . . they might have harmed you before that. Besides, alone and without my eyeglasses, I would likely never have reached any settlement." He blinked at the boy. "Anyway, I couldn't have left you alone, Tobias. I had to stay with you."

There was a loud honking cry overhead, and Mr. Twistletree paused to listen. "A great gray heron," he said, smiling a little to himself.

"Whonk, whonk, whonk," screamed the bird. And then in a little spell, much farther off, "Whonkee."

Mr. Twistletree sighed and seemed to collect himself. "But I cannot understand—Hummingbird let me believe all along that you were going with me," he went on.

"Injuns!" Tobe cried in hatred and rage and disappointment. "Whatever made you think you could trust the fool savages anyway? They're so natural-born blackhearted and mean, they'd as soon stab you in the back as look at you."

Mr. Twistletree rubbed his reddened eyes. "Listen, Tobias," he began. "Whatever happens, I want you to remember this. Indians are no more blackhearted than other folks. The white men are their enemies, and with good reason, at least the Indians think so. Whites have stolen their lands; they have taken their hunting grounds; they have given them their diseases. There's no place for the Indian to go. He can no longer find enough game to live on. He strikes out at the white man and his ways just as the rattlesnake strikes out at whatever he believes is menacing him. It is not you and me they hate and fear, Tobias, but whatever is new and strange. And that is the way with most men, especially ignorant ones."

Mr. Twistletree could talk all he was a mind to, preach till he was purple-headed. But he could never convince Tobias Bledsoe that Indians were less than devil-hearted.

Tobe moved to the far end of the cabin and sat in stony silence. He hoped his pa found out what had happened to him. Oh, he hoped Robert Bledsoe knew he'd as good as sold his son into Indian slavery! Not that it would matter. Pa had always thought more of hard money than of his own flesh and blood.

But his ma now—you'd think she would have spoken out when his father bound him to Asa Twistletree. You would think she'd have talked against him going off, much as she needed him and knowing full well Mr. Twistletree didn't have enough common sense to fill a peapod. She might have known things would end up this way.

In agony he got up and limped around and around the room. He would get away this very

night, he would; he had to. He wouldn't waste time thinking about his folks and getting mad at them; he'd figure out the best way to get out of here and back to the Holston. He would never let the Indians kill him.

He moved to the door and ran his fingers over the leather hinges. They were old and cracked in places but still good. It would take a heap of strength to wrench them loose. He pushed at the door, rattling the bar across the outside. It'd be a simple matter to dig away the chinking right beside the doorframe and reach out between the logs and push the bar loose.

Without another thought he began to claw away at the hard clay, digging and scraping till he had scrabbled his fingernails down to the quick and made no impressions on the clay at all. He gave up then and glanced at Mr. Twistletree. The naturalist slumped against the wall with one hand over his eyes.

"He's give up," thought Tobe. "He's give plumb up and it's up to me to get us out of here."

Tobe heard some horses gallop into town, and he ran from wall to wall, pressing his face against the logs and straining to see if it was the Canoe come home. He moaned a little to himself and wiped the sweat from his eyes. It would be just his luck for Dragging Canoe to come back right this minute before he'd had so much as one chance to get away. But it wasn't the chieftain, and there wasn't anybody

collecting wood for a fire either, nor did he see a stake anywhere.

He made himself sit down. He'd better take things easier; he was acting like a chicken with its head chopped off, a-flopping about this cabin. He didn't know what was the matter with him. It was so hot, but his hands and feet were cold. His breath came quick, for something seemed to press on his chest and keep him from getting a decent lungful of air.

There was still the roof. He'd forgotten the roof. It was the onliest way, the easiest way really. But he couldn't try it now in broad daylight. When it got good and dark, it'd be a simple matter to climb up the wall to the rafter and sit there while he pushed away the doty shingles.

Why, even Mr. Twistletree would be able to climb up that rough log wall! And once outside they could skedaddle to the creek that ran through the town, wade down it to the river, and swim across. Then the Indians would never find them, would never even know which way the two of them had gone.

Tobe waited a thousand years, crouched there by the wall, watching the blue dusk seep slow, slow, slowly into the cabin through the chinks and crannies. It was the hardest thing he'd ever had to do, wait in the middle of that Indian village, going over and over in his mind what he'd do, wondering if his plan would work, half afraid it might not and plumb terrified at what would happen if it didn't.

When at last it was dark enough, Tobe clambered up to the rafter, and in a few moments had a fair-sized hole. He stuck his head through it, and right away a dog barked. Below him a dim shape moved and he knew it was a guard. He could just make out the faint gleam of the rifle barrel, pointing upward.

For a moment he clung there, something in his throat jumping around like a cricket. He might have known there'd be a guard. Then he lowered himself back into the cabin and huddled in a corner. He lay there a long, long time without moving. Things had reached a point where he couldn't go on. He was so near dead already, he couldn't feel anything else. It didn't matter what happened to them. His family would never know how he'd died. And if they did find out, likely even Tildy wouldn't cry about it.

The next morning he was wearied out and a mite ashamed to have acted so. And yet at least he had tried. He hadn't just sat with his eyes closed and done nothing.

The new day's sun beat down on the cabin, and the coolness of the night began to drift away.

"Mr. Twistletree," Tobe whispered finally. "What do you aim for us to do? Ain't we going to try to get away? Just setting and waiting is more than a body can bear and that's the truth."

The man looked up. "Listen, Tobias," he answered, and his voice was suddenly stern. "Neither you nor I can escape from here. And if we did, likely they'd catch us before we could get back to the Holston. When you are stronger and I have my wits about me, our opportunity to get away will present itself."

Tobe stared.

"Don't despair; we'll find a way," the naturalist went on. "For the moment there's nothing for us to do but hope and pray. And if waiting is so painful for you, I will set you a task. It will help to pass the time."

Tobe opened his mouth to say he wouldn't do it. There wasn't any point to it. Knowing his letters wasn't going to be a heap of help to him when he was tied to that stake. Then he shrugged. He might as well. It was better than doing nothing, and it was easy seen Mr. Twistletree didn't have it in mind to try to escape.

For two days he fashioned his letters with a stick o the dirt floor and did sums just the way Mr. Twistree told him to. Oh, he was meek as Moses the whole time.

And it did keep him from worrying and fretting. The days went by quicker almost than any days he ever knew, and he didn't have time to ponder once over the Canoe or how it felt to stand on burning wood. He figured it must be like going to school, and when he lagged a bit, Mr. Twistletree's voice got a quick hard tone to it that kept him plugging right ahead.

At night when the cabin grew dark and Tobe began to feel scared and twitchity as a fox, the naturalist talked and told him stories. It was a living wonder what a heap of tales the man knew, stories out of the Bible and tales about strange Greek folks who thought they were gods and did some mighty queer things—tales about Greek warriors and Alexander the Great and Roman emperors and English kings, about that Richard who was called Lion-hearted and the other one with the crooked back, who was crueler than any Indian.

Mr. Twistletree could tell just aplenty about such folks, what kind of clothes they wore and what kind of food they ate, whether or not they had rifles to shoot with, and what kind of salves they used for their aches. Tobe reckoned he liked hearing about those other folks and their troubles better than anything.

The afternoon of the second day, Mr. Twistletree fell asleep. "Is this here how you spell it?" asked Tobe. When he got no answer, he turned to look. At first he thought his master was dead, he looked so white and his face was so drawn. But then he saw the naturalist was asleep.

Tobe stared at him for a few minutes, and it came over him suddenly that Mr. Twistletree was a brave man. He'd always figured being brave was going out and shooting a fierce bear or fighting Indians or redcoats. But now he could see that wasn't the only way for a man to have courage. It took a heap of grit and courage to stay here among the Chickamaugas, to give yourself up and sit in this cabin telling tales and adding figures when any minute you might be snatched up and torn to pieces.

"He done it for me," Tobe thought. "I reckon he would have give a power of money to leave here. It may be he was worried about his sister in Philadelphy. But he stayed here with me."

Nobody, not even his mam, had ever done so much for him before.

It would surprise his folks and Mr. Evans and the Cobbs, too, to know what a heap he thought of Mr. Twistletree. Skinny and sour-faced he might be, ignorant about how to use an ax or make a shelter, but he was a true friend and a brave man.

His mam wouldn't really be surprised. He remembered how she'd said, "Go with Mr. Twistletree; you might learn something." And he had. He'd found out that just because a body doesn't know the same things you know, it isn't certain proof he's a woodenhead.

And when he went to sleep that night, he dreamt he was walking through a green field with Tildy. She kept saying, "If'n Mr. Twistletree comes round, I'll fling this here rock at him and stew him for supper." But Mr. Twistletree never came.

"What I don't understand is how Injuns can get so fat on Injun food," Tobe said sadly the next morning. He crumbled a bit of the hard corn cake in his fingers. "Why this here stew and bread is enough to—"

He broke off. Somebody was coming closer. And somebody was opening the door. Tobe's heart came up in his throat and half stifled him.

It was the Hummingbird. He stood in the doorway with his green blanket wrapped close around him. Mr. Twistletree rose to his feet and spoke very civilly.

Tobe said nothing. The corn bread was stuck in his craw. Was this the time they would be taken out and killed? What else would the Hummingbird have come for?

The Indian was silent too. He looked all around the cabin and took another step inside the room.

"What's he slippy-sliding around for, that-a-way?" Tobe asked himself. The medicine man was up to something. There was a queer look about him. Tobe couldn't lay a finger on it, but it was different from the way the old Indian had been before.

The Hummingbird moved closer to Mr. Twistletree and then stepped back. His face worked a minute and finally he said, "Many warriors go to treaty. Many go to Creek town." He stopped and blinked a little. "Traders gone."

He paused again and seemed to be waiting for Mr. Twistletree to understand what he meant. "Interpreter gone," he added glumly. He pulled one hand out from his blanket and held up a dirty piece of paper. "Hummingbird not know what talking paper say. Dumb Injun bring paper . . . him not know what say." He gave the paper an angry shake.

"White man know," he cried suddenly. "White man tell what talking paper say."

He thrust the letter into Mr. Twistletree's hand. The naturalist took it and turned it over slowly, holding it up close to his face. There was a big ragged red seal on it.

"Now," thought Tobe. "Now's our chance. This here's the opportunity Mr. Twistletree's been talking about. He can tell old Hummingbird anything, anything in creation. He can say John Sevier is coming down here with a thousand men to wipe out this town, lessen we're set free. He can say William Bartram is sending a wagon load of ax heads and silver shillings to ransom us. Oh, he's got that old Injun in a cleft stick."

"It is your letter," Mr. Twistletree began. "Right here it says: 'To the Hummingbird at Running Water Town.'"

The old man nodded. Tobe grinned deep inside himself. That was the way to do. That already made Hummingbird sit up and take notice, getting a letter sent right smack to him that way. Oh, his master could be evermore sly when the time came for it!

Mr. Twistletree broke the red wax seal and unfolded the paper. "Here is the message," he began.

"To the Hummingbird at Running Water Town:

I am sorry that you were not able to come to

the treaty meeting at White's Fort on the Holston. We are the losers by your absence. But I still hold your friendship very dear. The peace that exists between my people and your people gladdens my heart. To strengthen our handclasp, I am sending you a fine red coat and two dozen gold buttons. Let us walk together on the path of friendship always.

(Signed) William Blount"

Tobe gave a quick gasp, and the last crumb of his corn bread went down the wrong way. He choked and sputtered and coughed till the tears ran down his face. He limped over to the water bucket and took a long drink, letting the water trickle down over his chin and neck.

He set the piggin down smartly. And how many such opportunities did Mr. Twistletree reckon he was going to get, he asked himself angrily? Didn't he see that this was the very time to scare the blanket off the old medicine man? How come he hadn't told him James Robertson was just over the ridge waiting to burn the town if he didn't let the white prisoners go? Oh, there were a thousand clever ways Mr. Twistletree could have tricked the Hummingbird if he'd only tried!

The old Indian reached over and took the letter. He looked at it carefully, inside and out, rubbing a big thumb over the writing. At last he glanced up into Mr. Twistletree's face, and his little eyes grew harder than ever.

"White man got forked tongue," he blazed out suddenly. "White man lie!"

Mr. Twistletree drew himself up very straight and grew red as a turkey cock. "You have asked me to read your letter," he said curtly. "I have done so. Keep your letter. When the interpreter comes back, let him read it. And *then* say that William Bartram's friend has lied to you, if you can!"

The Hummingbird frowned. He turned the letter over and over, holding it up close to his nose as the white man had done. Once he ran a finger along under the words, screwing up his face and looking worried.

"He don't know whether to jump or stand still," Tobe thought, studying the old man. He hoped he never got in such a sorry plight.

Nobody ever wrote him a letter. But supposing somebody did, could he read it? Or would he have to ask some other body to do it for him? And could he trust that other body?

"White man not lie?" the Hummingbird asked finally. "Not tell poor Injun lie?"

"I have not spoken any word but the truth since I came here," Mr. Twistletree answered angrily. "Only truth can be spoken between the friends of William Bartram. I have said I was in your territory gathering plants. I have said I did wrong to come, but I have done no harm to anybody. My bound boy has done no harm. We came in peace and we wish to leave with peace always between us."

The old medicine man turned and stared at Tobe, and the boy looked sullenly back.

"Listen, ha!" the Hummingbird said sharply. "Old ways change much. Young brave laugh at old man . . . not hear what Hummingbird say. Hummingbird say . . . sing hunting song when you kill deer. Young men not sing . . . deer all gone. Young men laugh, not listen . . . kill snakes, steal guns, do wicked. Dragging Canoe not hear Hummingbird . . . not listen to old man. Bad times for Injuns, much trouble."

He looked almost sad. His shoulders sagged, and he seemed to grow smaller as if something inside of him was shrinking and drying up.

"Now Governor Blount be angry because Hummingbird take white prisoners. Chucky Jack be much mad . . . make war on Injuns. Hummingbird sorry for war . . . sorry for killing."

He was silent for a long spell. He seemed to be listening to something way off in the distance. "White man friend of Hummingbird," he said finally. "Him tell truth like William Bartram tell truth. Hummingbird let prisoners go, let white man go . . . let white boy go back to Phil'delphy. Hwi-la-hi. Go, then!"

Fourteen

Tobe couldn't help running. Even though the sun was so hot and he hadn't exactly had a gracious plenty to eat the past few days, he couldn't help trotting up ahead. Their Indian guide had been left long ago at the peaceful Cherokee town of Chota. And Tobe and Mr. Twistletree had crossed to the north bank of the Holston River and were once again on the trail the two of them had traveled last March, a good four months back.

And here it was almost August and he was almost home. Home! His duty done, his time served out with Mr. Twistletree. Oh, wasn't it almighty good to be free, not cooped up like a broody hen any longer?

He didn't wait for Mr. Twistletree to catch up with him but went running back.

"You know what?" he cried. "One thing I've learned for a fact, a body that can use his two legs to go about where he pleases has got a mighty valuable thing. If'n I ever own a dog, I ain't *never* going to tie him up."

Mr. Twistletree smiled. "Too often we don't appreciate what we have until we lose it, Tobias," he said. "Fortunately we regained our liberty, but I hope you ne'er forget what a prized possession it is." He blinked down at the trail and rubbed his eyes.

"I wisht we could of got your spectacles back—though I reckon you'd rather have the ledger book," Tobe suggested.

Mr. Twistletree nodded slowly. "Yes, it's a great loss to me. But never mind. I can remember many things. And perhaps someday I'll have a chance to return to the fort."

Tobe was astonished. "Return!" he repeated. "You mean go back there and likely git caught again? You might not get away next time."

"No. No, perhaps not," answered Mr. Twistletree, and he sighed. "I would like to talk to Hummingbird again, however. He could teach me many things about Cherokee customs and tell me more stories about the Thunder Boys and the Boiling Pot in the river. I would dearly love to know about the medicinal plants and herbs the old fellow had hanging in his hut. Who knows what cures the Indians may not have devised?"

The naturalist stopped and looked ready to turn around and go back to Running Water.

"I reckon he just might do it," Tobe thought as they began to walk on. It was queer. When he set out with Mr. Twistletree, he'd thought learning was just a way of getting out of work, or a weakness in the head. And then he'd begun to think it was like the little bits of colored pebbles and flowers Tildy used to play with in the creek—something bright colored and gay to pleasure one's self with. When Mr. Twistletree used to sit and watch beetles or get out his bird skins and look them over, Tobe had often been reminded of Tildy putting a white pebble and a blue violet on a piece of moss.

But it wasn't like that really. It was like—it was like walking in new country, when every time you saw a hill you wanted to know what lay beyond it, and when every bend in a strange river was the bend you just had to go around and see what kind of country was there. It was a far frontier just waiting for somebody to lay claim to it, learning was.

Tobe knew how it was himself. A body no sooner learned three times seven than he wanted to know what three times eight was. He no sooner knew about Crook-Back Richard than he wanted to know about Lion-Hearted Richard.

"I wish," he said suddenly, "when my granny wanted to teach me my letters out of the Bible when I was just a little feller, my pappy had let her."

"No doubt your pa thought he was doing the right thing," Mr. Twistletree replied. "Down here in this woodland country men need to know how to shoot and hunt, how to use an ax and a knife, more than other skills. But there ought to be some learning in every place. Men will always need lawyers and doctors and schoolteachers. As soon as fields are cleared and cabins built, then you have to have men to make laws and keep accounts, to learn the news and tell it out, to write letters and teach."

It was true, Tobe knew it was. How come his pa hadn't been able to see that not being able to read was like being locked up in a log cabin, like having walls all around yourself? A body who couldn't even read his own letters was a kind of prisoner, the same as if he'd been an Indian slave.

Tobe grinned a little. "I wonder will old Hummingbird ever get his red coat," he remarked.

The naturalist smiled. "I hope so," he answered. "I hope to send some gifts to the Hummingbird myself, for I'm almost certain that he had to pay some ransom for us, since he was not the one who captured us. I would like to know he was repaid."

"It was smart, the way you handled the old man," Tobe said, a little shyly. "I made sure you'd try to scare him into letting us go. I figured you'd lie about the letter."

Mr. Twistletree shook his head. "No, no, I didn't want to do that. It might have worked with another Indian—or another white man," he added wryly. "No, I could see that the Hummingbird wanted to let us go. He was afraid, for one thing. The town was well-nigh defenseless with so many gone to the treaty-making. He didn't want to make any trouble that might cause the white men to attack Running Water."

He stopped, fanning himself with a big leaf. "And more than that, he was ashamed to have William Bartram's white friends think that his red friend was less honest and generous than they were."

"Well, how come he didn't let me go right away?" Tobe asked, moving on again beside the naturalist. "How come him to hold me and give out all that about rattlesnakes?"

"I think he really believes anybody who killed a rattlesnake was doing wrong," Mr. Twistletree said. "Probably a very ancient belief, one of those he complained that nobody but him observed any more."

"Like those young men not listening to him?" asked Tobe.

"Yes," agreed the naturalist soberly. "I think the Hummingbird knows the Indians' day is done. Dragging Canoe is not really bringing back the old ways to the red man as he promised. He is only prolonging a dreadful war. The Hummingbird is too wise not to see this plainly, and he was trying to tell us that he regrets having joined forces with the Chickamaugas. Much as he would love to see the Indians restored to their former power and their lands returned, he knows it cannot be, and he is sorry that so much suffering has come about for a vain cause."

"Looky yonder, Mr. Twistletree," cried Tobe. "There's the turning off path to our cabin. I'm plumb home!"

"Well," Mr. Twistletree stopped and looked pleased. "I'm glad to see it, Tobias, glad indeed. When I set out with you, I did not know how often we would walk in the shadow of death. But here you are returned safely and I rejoice."

Tobe was a little flustered. "You done your best for me," he answered. "There ain't any place to go in the woods and not run a chance of getting killed."

"There's . . . there's a thing I want to . . . I must ask you, boy," Mr. Twistletree went on.

His voice rasped out, and Tobe looked at him, wondering what could make him stammer around so.

There was a long pause. "Tobias," said Mr. Twistletree at last. "Come to Philadelphia with me. I can teach you many things—Latin and Greek and mathematics. History too. In the winter months I tutor several lads your age, and none of them is any quicker than you. You could help me in the school, and in the summer you could go with me to gather herbs and study plants in the woods. You could hunt then."

Tobe stared. It was the last thing in the world he'd expected Mr. Twistletree to say. It took him by surprise, for a fact.

He'd like to go. It would be fine to have a trade so a body wouldn't have to roam around the way his pa did, to be able to read and write, and to know a heap of things.

But he couldn't go. His ma needed him, and all the rest of the family. He had to do the hunting and farming. He had to be the steady one when his pap was off on some wild scheme. Besides, he was not a town boy. He'd never learn their ways.

He shook his head. "I'd like to," he said regretfully. "But I reckon my family kind of depends on me a heap."

They turned off along the path, and Tobe noticed how grown up it looked, as though his folks kept to themselves and didn't go walking along it much.

"I'm a-going to learn to read, though. I'll git somebody to help me," he promised.

"I hope you do, Tobias," said Mr. Twistletree. "I'm sorry we must part, you and I."

"I reckon my folks must be using another spring," said Tobe uneasily. "The path to the old one has well-nigh gone, it's got so many weeds in it."

They walked on. And they almost walked past the cabin. The roof had gone at one corner and the bushes had grown up so tall and green round about that it was half-hidden. Tobe's heart sank. A body didn't need to push open the door to see it was empty. It gave him a queer feeling to see the fireboard as bare as your hand and not even ashes on the hearth.

The Bledsoes had gone.

"Tobias!" squeaked Mr. Twistletree. "Where are your parents? What do you intend to do?"

Tobe stood a minute thinking. It was a shock. But

he might have known they'd be gone. His pap was never one to stay put, especially if he had money in his pocket.

He wouldn't say that to Mr. Twistletree. "Likely they've moved to a new cabin," he said slowly. "Haymores' place is nearest. I reckon my mammy left a message with the Haymores."

All the way there he kept turning over in his mind all the possibilities. Maybe they'd gone back to Nashville or down to Spanish territory with the Cobbs and Mr. Evans. He didn't think that was it. Mr. Evans would know he had troubles enough with the Cobbs and his own six girls, without the Bledsoes along. Or maybe to Salisbury where his uncle lived.

They took a short cut through the fields to Haymores'. "I'll wait for you here," Mr. Twistletree said as they stood at the edge of the clearing. "I do not think Mistress Haymore has a good opinion of me."

Tobe nodded. He recalled the scalding water. "There ain't no need to wait," Tobe told him. "Mrs. Haymore will know where they are. You'd best go on."

Mr. Twistletree looked worried. "I feel that I ought to take you back to your parents," he stated. "It isn't right just to leave you like this."

"Supposing they've done gone back to Nashville," Tobe answered shortly. "You ain't fixing to take me clean over to *Nashville*. There's good traveling time left this day, Mr. Twistletree. You'd best go on. I can take care of myself, and that's a fact."

"Ah, I know it well, Tobias," the man agreed. "You're a good boy and a capable one. I'll take my leave then. You've been a help to me in many ways and I thank you. If our journey came to naught, there's no help for it, is there? I bid you good day."

"Fare-thee-well, Mr. Twistletree," said Tobe. He stood and watched the man going along the path. It was a good journey to Philadelphia. But it was all over fine roads, wide and well-traveled. Mr. Twistletree would get along all right. It might even be some wagoner would give him a ride. "If'n I ever get to Philadelphy, I'll come to see you," he shouted.

Mr. Twistletree turned and waved a hand to show he'd heard and, though Tobe knew well enough the man couldn't see him, he waved back.

Mrs. Haymore was round in the back, and a heap of little Haymores were there too. "Well, Tobe," she called out when she saw him. "I had you in mind all this day. Your mam figured you'd be back close to this time."

"Where are they at?" Tobe blurted out, forgetting his manners.

"They've gone to Kentuck," she answered. "Gone to a salt lick up near Harrod's Fort."

Tobe stood there, fumbling at the old Indian musket he'd been given by the Hummingbird. "Didn't she say . . . didn't they leave me no word?" he asked at last.

"Sal, git them young 'uns away from that fire!"
hollered Mrs. Haymore. "Your mam left word.
Said you was to come if you was a mind to."

Tobe swallowed. It wasn't the kind of word he
had thought to get. "If you was a mind to." It
sounded for all the world like they didn't want him
or need him but figured it was mannerly to ask him
along.

It made him a little angry. He hadn't chosen to
go with Mr. Twistletree in the first place. But more
than that, he'd counted a heap on getting back here
and helping them out. And now they didn't want
his help.

Well, he'd go after them. He didn't have any
other place to go whether they wanted him or not.

"You can stay with us, Tobe, till you're rested
up," Mrs. Haymore said kindly.

"I thank ye," muttered the boy. "I'll work for my
keep."

Sally Haymore came up and giggled at him.
"You look like you been eating old Twistletree's
Latin lessons," she said. "You're skinny as he was
nearabouts. I reckon you're glad to see the last of
him, ain't you?"

"Glad enough," Tobe answered briefly. "Gimme
that piggin. I'll fetch your ma some water."

Billy Haymore was down at the spring torment-
ing crawdads. He jumped up when he saw Tobe
and crowed with laughter. "There was a heap of
folks around here said you'd never get back alive,"

he cried. "How'd you keep off the buzzards—fight 'em with them eye-speckles or whatever you call 'em?"

"No buzzards come around," Tobe retorted. "They was all up here looking for you."

"Aw, I reckon you had some kind of trouble," Billy went on. "I reckon an old addlepate like Twistletree runs into trouble pretty regular."

"We had some mishaps," Tobe replied pulling up the dripping bucket. "But I wouldn't say it was Mr. Twistletree's doing." He walked off and left Billy.

That night Mr. Haymore asked him about Asa Twistletree. "I told your pappy I didn't think it was right for him to bind you out to that man," Mr. Haymore announced self-righteously. "That feller wasn't right in the head. It was plumb dangerous to send you off with him."

"Naw," Tobe spoke up quickly. "He ain't like you think. He's . . . he's different from what he looks like." He thought a minute. "It ain't as bad as you think to know all them things he knows."

"Well, it's all well and good for you to say that," Mr. Haymore went on. "But what you reckon would of happened if'n you'd run into Injun trouble? Book learning wouldn't of helped you there."

"Well, it *did*," Tobe muttered. But he didn't say any more. He wasn't going to tell the Haymores all that had happened. It wasn't any use in the first place. He'd never be able to make them understand about Mr. Twistletree. Maybe he couldn't stand up and shoot Indians and bears and catamounts, but he was brave, just the same. He was a good man too. And he got along pretty well with the Chickamaugas, a heap better than most white men. At any rate, he'd got the two of them away alive.

And how come the Haymores were so dead set against book learning? Mr. Haymore had lost a big farm up in Kentuck because he hadn't been able to get a proper deed drawn up. And Mrs. Haymore had a crook in her right arm from getting it hurt and not having a doctor to fix it. You'd think they'd both be willing to see somebody get a little learning.

You'd think—Tobe stopped suddenly. What had his ma said? "Come to Kentuck if you're a mind to." What was his mam trying to tell him? Was she saying, "You're old enough now to know your own mind and make your own choices. If'n you don't want to be like Mr. Haymore, don't be."

He was quick, Mr. Twistletree had told him so. He could learn a heap of things besides how to mold a bullet and how to make a fire. He could be a doctor or a teacher and come to live on the Holston where folks needed such men. He could do—no telling what he could do!

He stood up suddenly. "I won't be here long to trouble you," he said politely to Mr. Haymore. "I reckon I'll be leaving tomorrow. I aim to bust out of here like the cold hives. How far do you reckon it is to Philadelphy?"

AUTHOR'S NOTE

This story takes place in 1791, when Tennessee existed as the Territory South of the River Ohio. William Blount was the governor, and he did hold a treaty with the Cherokee and Chickamauga Indians in July of that year at what is now Knoxville. Although Governor Blount wrote letters to the Indians and sometimes sent them presents, I have had to invent the letter from him in Chapter Thirteen.

Asa Twistletree is modeled on several of the early naturalists, men whose love of books and learning, whose zeal for discovery and whose passion for all of nature stands out clear and sharp on every page of their journals. So he has some characteristics of William Bartram, of Constantine Rafinesque, of Alexander Wilson, and of André Michaux, but it has been beyond my talents to capture here the "sunny glory" that was Audubon.

In his "Travels" William Bartram speaks often of his Cherokee friends, though he does not mention one named the Hummingbird.

The old fort described in Chapter Nine stands near Manchester, Tennessee, today.